I0641133

Tom Bevan

The Thane of the Dean

A tale of the time of the conqueror

Tom Bevan

The Thane of the Dean
A tale of the time of the conqueror

ISBN/EAN: 9783337027056

Printed in Europe, USA, Canada, Australia, Japan

Cover: Foto ©Andreas Hilbeck / pixelio.de

More available books at **www.hansebooks.com**

THE

THANE OF THE DEAN.

A TALE OF THE TIME OF THE CONQUEROR.

BY

TOM BEVAN.

WITH FOUR ILLUSTRATIONS BY LANCELOT SPEED.

LONDON:

S. W. PARTRIDGE & CO.,

8 & 9, PATERNOSTER ROW.

1899

CONTENTS.

THANE OF THE DEAN.

CHAPTER I.

IN WHICH THE SONS OF WULF RIDE TO GLOUCESTER.

I N the evening of a December day, A.D. 1083, two boys emerged from the darkness of the thick Forest which lay between the rivers Wye and Severn, and stood upon the high western bank of the latter river. The point at which they stood was the outermost one in the great semi-circular sweep which the river makes about twelve miles below the ancient city of Gloucester. The small river-township of Newnham-on-Severn now clusters round this point ; at the time of our story a few mud fisher-cabins lined the shore above the high-tide mark, and the low, rambling, wooden house of " Orcar-of-the-Forest-edge " capped the summit of the shoreward incline at the spot where now stands the parish church.

The sun had sunk to rest behind the leafless mass of thick forest nearly an hour ago, and but for the clear light of the young moon, and the reflection from a landscape lightly powdered over with frozen snow, the darkness in this shadow of the Forest would have been intense.

One glance at the two lads would have conveyed to the observer the intelligence that they were of good, probably noble, birth. Each was dressed in a woollen tunic edged with fur and girt at the waist with a broad leathern belt. Daylight would have shown that the tunic was deep blue in colour, and that the fur came from the back of the beaver. "Trews," or trousers, of a light-coloured woollen material, cross-gartered from ankle to knee with strips of tanned deerskin, clothed their legs, deerskin shoes encased their feet, a short cloak covered their shoulders, and a round cap of beaver-fur sat jauntily on each curly, flaxen head. Appearance and dress proclaimed them brothers.

"Well, Edwy," exclaimed the elder of the two lads, "there thou hast the great river before thee."

"I would then that the great river kept a supply of water more worthy its name," exclaimed Edwy, with a shrug. "Unless mine eyes and the moonshine befool me, one has need to stretch one's legs across enough of sand before the water of the river is reached. 'Tis a poor show for so great a name."

The elder brother laughed merrily. "In good sooth," cried he, "it was high time our lady-mother allowed thee to wander abroad beyond the small space of land within the glance of her dear eyes. I must crave more freedom for thee, or thou wilt grow up either hermit or bower-maiden, and such fate must never befall a son of Wulf."

"Such fate is not for me!" answered the younger

lad with an indignant blush. "Thou art unkind, brother Gurth, to make a jest of mine ignorance."

"Nay, nay, thou must not begrudge me my jest, little brother, if I purpose to turn thine ignorance to deepest wisdom," said Gurth kindly. He placed his arm on his brother's shoulder and drew him closer to his side.

"Let me begin to school thee at once," continued he. "Before the robin shall pipe its first song to-morrow, or the first red rays of the sun glint along this bank, the river will be full and foaming from bank to bank. Yon small, mud-coloured stream thou so cavillest at shall spread itself deep o'er all these bare sands, and that, too, in less time than it shall take thee to run thrice round the meadow that fronts our mother's house. Faster will the sea rush up than thy small legs can carry thee across the spring green-sward. 'Tis then the fisher-folk spread their nets to catch the great salmon for the thane Orcar; and I have heard men say that sometimes huge whales come thus far, borne in upon the bosom of the mighty tide."

"Then assuredly," broke in Edwy enthusiastically, "at such a time should they call the Severn 'the great river!'" He paused for a moment, then added, "Brother, I would fain see this coming-in of the sea; with thy good leave I will stay here this night and watch for it."

"Not to-night! Not to-night!" said Gurth good-humouredly, as he patted Edwy's flushed cheek, "but thou shalt have thy wish ere thou behold our lady-mother's face again. I promise thee thou shalt not go back lacking of tales of wonder for her ears, and for the ears of our bonny Editha. But now we must to the house of Orcar, to crave sup and shelter for the night. We have a long ride awaiting us before the noon of to-morrow."

The two lads turned away from the river and walked towards the edge of the nearest belt of trees, where they had tethered their sturdy little ponies, having walked them down the last part of the dark and ill-defined woodland track. They untied their shaggy steeds, and each took a javelin from his saddle-bow before commencing a brisk walk up the moonlit slope towards their destination.

This Orcar to whom they went was one of the lesser Saxon thanes, a great burly fellow, who spent his time according to season and circumstance in the varied occupations of fishing the Severn for its salmon, cultivating a narrow belt of rich soil, feeding swine in the glades of the oak forest, resisting the incursions of the neighbouring Welsh, or, joining forces with the dependants of the great thane Wulf, attacking in his turn these restless and ruthless marauders; time and continual occupation hardly permitted any quarrel of moment with his Saxon neighbours. The Welsh usually gave these border thanes, or thanes of the Marches, a thoroughly satisfactory allowance of fighting.

The two lads seeking the shelter of his roof were the orphan sons of his late neighbour and. ally, the great thane, "Wulf of the Dean." The thane himself, whose very name had long been a source of terror to the Welsh, had fallen, in the prime of his manhood, at the hand of these dauntless and untiring foes. To Edwy, his father was no more than the idolised hero of an oft-told, stirring tale—the brave knight of the romance which enshrouded his mother's heart. He was born some few months after his father's death, and coming at such a time to check the torrent of his mother's bitter grief, he was beloved by her above her other children, and watched and guarded with such an anxious solicitude that his brother Gurth often feared whether he would grow to that sturdy manhood which should be expected in a son of the brave Wulf.

Gurth himself was a straight and lithesome stripling of some seventeen summers, the veritable right hand of his still young and handsome mother, who, since the death of her husband, had guarded, with an excellent judgment and wisdom, the destinies and welfare of her little forest realm in the Dean.

Beloved by them of low degree, respected and honoured by the powerful and turbulent spirits around her, no worldly matters had suffered at her hands, so that Gurth bid fair to succeed to a goodly and well-preserved heritage.

The gossips said, that during her twelve years of widowhood more than one worthy gentleman had made an offer of heart, and life, and limb, in her sole service; but all such offers were courteously and firmly declined. Her life was devoted to the memory of her husband, and to the noble task of rearing his two sons, so that they might emulate the renown of so worthy and devoted a sire.

Often had rumour linked her name with that of the

thane Orcar. Truly her station was above his; yet it had not always been so, for the gallant Wulf had wooed and won his bonny bride from the hut of a freeman forester on his ancestral lands. Certain it was that Orcar was always her trusted adviser, ever her first help in time of need, and never having had wife or child of his own, he had bestowed no small meed of his affection on the Lady of the Dean and her three children. Especially had he watched with kindly and friendly eye the life and fortunes of the gallant young Gurth.

Let us now accompany the sons of Wulf to the house of the burly and generous thane.

They soon ascended the winding path to the summit of the low hill, and found themselves at the narrow plank-bridge which crossed the artificial ditch or moat and led immediately to the high palisade or outer fortifications of Orcar's house. The passage of the bridge was an easy matter in the bright moonlight, but on reaching the oaken gate of the palisade they found it firmly locked and barred. Gurth struck it sharply several times with the butt end of his javelin, and an armed henchman soon appeared and demanded their name and errand.

" Gurth, son of Wulf, craves entrance to the house of Orcar ! " answered the elder lad sharply.

The fellow on hearing this was hastening to the gate, murmuring confused apologies for the " poor light of the moon," and his " weakening sight," when Orcar himself appeared from within upon the threshold of his house. He recognised the newcomers instantly, and hastened forward to give them hearty greeting.

"Welcome to ye, my sons!" cried he, shaking both vigorously by the hand. "I have awaited your coming all day. Come in ; the red glare of good oaken logs will suit ye better this December eve than the cold light of yon moon."

Thanking the good thane for his kindness, the lads left their ponies with the servitor, and entered the house. They followed their host into a long, well-lighted room, whose wooden walls and low, black roof were fashioned from the heart of the neighbouring forest. Great oaken pillars—which were nothing better nor worse than entire trunks of something like uniform size stripped of their bark— supported the heavily raftered roof throughout its entire length.

Across one end of the room a bountiful supper was laid on smooth, well-scrubbed planks, quite innocent of table-cloth and supported on roughly fashioned trestles. In the centre of the hard, earthen, rush-strewn floor burned a great fire of pine and oaken logs, the pungent smoke from which rolled lazily and cloudily upwards, spread itself abroad among the sooty rafters, or found its way into the bright winter air through a circular hole in the highest ridge of the roof. Near the fire were two large settles, and to these Orcar led his young guests. When the two lads were seated, one on either side of their worthy host, the latter began a round of questions.

"Well, Edwy," cried he merrily, and stroking the youngster's curls, "so thy good mother hath now sent thee out amongst the sons of men. Dost think thou wilt hold thine own with them ? And what hast thou purposed to do with the hungry wolf and the tusked boar ? Didst meet no giant in thy path to-day, and did none of the pretty wenches from the pages of thy books cry out to thee for succour ? "

"I met no wolf, nor bear, nor maiden," answered the lad ; "and as to thy other questions, good thane, I'll answer them anon."

"And how wilt thou answer them ? " asked the old thane affectionately.

"By no words," replied the lad quietly, "but by deeds, when time and chance shall serve me ! "

"An answer worthy of thy blood ! " cried Orcar. "Ah ! thou art true son of Wulf ! I thought thy gentle mother was like to make a milksop of thee. She hath too much wit. The gods pardon me for my unjust thoughts ! "

The rough old fellow took their hands kindly in his own. " I love ye well ! " he said, "for ye are good and worthy lads ; and well may ye be so, for ye had for sire a good and worthy man. That he was gentle, your mother's still green love for him doth prove. Just was he—his vassals love his memory now. Of his brave deeds let his enemies speak ; no axe bit deeper than the axe of the Wulf, and no sword flashed brighter in the thickest fray. Staunch was he in friend-ship as true maid in love ; of that no man may speak more than myself. And of your mother I will say but this,—no king's babe ever nestled to a nobler heart ! Nobly were ye reared, nobly must ye do ! "

He turned to Gurth. "Now tell me of this journey to Gloucester. What takes ye thither at such a time, and why doth Edwy brave the dangers

of the road? Methinks his first journey should
have been a lighter one."

"If it please thee, good thane, I would rather
tell thee after we have supped," answered Gurth.
"It is not a matter for ears other than thine own;"
and he glanced at the "house-carles" who were
assembling for the evening meal.

"So be it," replied the thane. "We will to
table now."

Orcar at once gave the signal for all to be
seated; and eating and drinking were soon the
order of the hour. Meat there was in plenty, for
the Forest supplied game of every sort, from the
bristly boar and the noble stag down to the humble
hare and small wild fowl. There was but little
river fish. For drink the men had mead and beer,
and the boys sparkling water from the cold spring
that bubbled up in the rear courtyard of Orcar's
house.

Before the repast was over, Edwy, despite his
strange surroundings, began to nod with sleepiness.
House-carles of Orcar were excellent trenchermen;
they ate largely and drank deeply, and were in
no hurry to quit the table. Moreover, there was
ample matter for wordy discussion, and their talk
soon became animated and loud-voiced.

Firstly, the Norman king was at Gloucester;
would he come to the Forest to hunt as he had
done before? There were stories to be told of his
last hunting. Was not the young Gurth, their
master's guest of to-night, born when the king
hunted the Forest seventeen summers ago? Secondly,

a band of daring Welsh had crossed the Wye, and were reported to be lurking in the Forest. Thirdly, the high tides were expected in a couple of days when the December moon would be full. Fourthly, Yuletide was at hand, and there was much to be said on that point. Orcar and Gurth said but little ; they had food for ample thought.

Supper, however, like all earthly matters, came at length to an end. The house-carles dispersed to their various posts and duties, the servitors cleared the tables, and the two lads and the old thane were once more alone. Edwy, tired out by the unwonted length of his journey, had fallen fast asleep, his head nestled on his brother's knee. Gurth at once took up the conversation, and answered the questions Orcar had put to him immediately before supper.

Said he, " Thou wouldst know, good thane, why I go to Gloucester at this season, and why Edwy goes with me? The reasons are these. Thou knowest the Norman, Gilbert of Tournay, whom the king hath granted lands adjoining mine, and thou knowest how he doth pursue my mother with offers of marriage and alliance—offers which she from her soul abhors, not only because he is a foreigner and an usurping tyrant, but because of his wicked nature and of the evil which report speaks of him. Well, latterly hath he grown insupportable. His vassals are for ever interfering with ours, and, if we make complaint of their encroachments, it is ever the same remedy that he doth propose, namely, that my mother should wed with him and unite their houses. That will she never do ! "

"God forbid!" interrupted Orcar angrily.

"This present moon," continued Gurth, "he hath taken to openly deride, insult, and threaten us, incited thereto no doubt by his known favour with the king and the near presence of the Normans at Gloucester.

"I would have gone out against him," he cried, and his eyes flashed as he spoke, "for the men of our house are many and brave, and the stout smiths and miners of Cinderford are sworn vassals of the house of Wulf. We could have thrust his insults down his craven throat. My mother, however, forbade. She said it was the way to lose all, and maybe bring upon her the dread fate which hath befallen so many noble Saxon dames. Better was it, she advised, to seek audience of the king, and lay our cause before him. My sire was no enemy of his after the Witan crowned him king, and when he hunted near us at the time of my birth, he stayed with us, swore friendship with us, spoke my sire fair, and vowed that as we had loyally served him, so would he royally repay us. Besides this, our house hath claims upon him, in that we have kept this border securely from the Welsh for many years. I have told thee all, thane. Dost thou not think my purpose good?"

"Good as may be! Good as may be! Yet would I rather that we took this Norman by the beard, and taught him the respect due to defenceless Saxon ladies. But the gods are ever good, Gurth; the time shall yet come when thou and I may stand within yon fellow's new-built walls and read him such sharp

2

counsel as he needs. Try thou thy luck at present
with the king. Men speak of him as stark and cruel,
yet I hold that he is not altogether unjust. Certain
is it that he is not unwise. Therefore do I think he
will speak the son of Wulf fair, for the Forest is a
troublesome way from London, and it would be well
for him to make firm friends of men tried and
strong, who live in the hearts of the western folk,
and who can keep their acres and his from the hands
of those thieving Welsh."

"My mind is as thine, good thane, on that matter,"
answered Gurth, "and it is in this tried service of
our house and in the love the people bear us that
I place hopes of success for my plea."

Orcar made no further remark for the moment, but
sat watching the ruddy glow of the firelight as it
danced and flickered and wavered upon the golden
curls of the sleeping Edwy. He placed his hand
caressingly on the boy's head, and turning again to
the elder brother asked, almost whisperingly, "But
why goes the lad with thee, and why do ye journey
alone and unguarded? Surely this is not thy mother's
plan?"

"No," answered Gurth with a smile, "it is not;
yet it hath her approval. Thou knowest there is
little danger for us in the Forest, and for the rest
of the journey I purposed showing the king how I
relied upon his presence to keep the neighbourhood
free from the enemies of law and order. I would show
him that I trust in him and in his power."

The old thane smiled grimly too. "Thou art
paying him a pretty compliment," he said, "and I

doubt not that thy faith will stand thee in good stead."

For some time longer Gurth and his old friend sat chatting by the winter firelight. Many things had Orcar to ask of Gurth concerning his mother's estate, the behaviour and well-doing of her vassals, retainers, and servitors. Anxious too was he concerning the young Edwy—how the lad shaped in athletic exercises and warlike sports ; his health, strength, and powers of endurance. And much sage advice did he give to the noble-spirited and adventurous lad—how he should conduct himself before the king, both as vassal and as the leading man of the proud and powerful house of Wulf.

The hour of bedtime—an early one—at length came, and soon afterwards the house of Orcar was wrapped in sleep and silence.

The next morning broke bright and sunny, and the lads were astir betimes. After a hearty breakfast they mounted their wiry little Forest ponies, and, accompanied by the old thane, rode on their way north-eastwards to the city.

Much as Orcar approved of Gurth's policy of appealing to the kingly vanity of the Conqueror by his unguarded ride, yet he could not but see that considerable risk was being run, and so, on pretext of a morning gallop in their company, he proposed to ride with them a part of the way. The lads were mightily pleased at the prospect, and it was a merry party that started off along the river-side road. The old thane made the way merry with many a story, and in less than two hours they stood at the ford of that branch of the Severn which encircles the western side of the island of Olney.

Here, after listening to a few last words of advice, the lads parted from Orcar, and, fording the shallow river, sped along the island causeway towards the turrets and towers which rose against the blue-grey winter sky before them. The thane watched them until they disappeared in the distance amongst the heavy farmers' wains labouring towards the city with good things for the tables and stables of the king, the abbot, and the worthy citizens. Then he turned and rode sharply homewards, purposing to send a speedy messenger to the Lady of the Dean announcing the safe arrival of her sons at their destination.

CHAPTER II.

CROSSING the river again at the other side of the island, the lads entered the city at the western gate and ascended the sloping Westgate Street in the direction of the abbey, at which place the Conqueror was at present lodged. They had no intention of seeking the royal presence at so early an hour, their present object being merely the satisfaction of their curiosity—or rather the satisfaction of the curiosity of Edwy, for Gurth was no stranger to the sights and sounds of Gloucester.

Yet even he found plenty to attract his attention this sharp December morning. The street was thronged with bustling life. Stalwart men-at-arms appeared everywhere, pages hurried to and fro on their masters' errands, cowled and sandalled monks wandered outside the precincts of the beautiful abbey, sturdy citizens stood at their doors or chatted with their neighbours in the roadway, many a bright girlish face looked out from the upper windows of the quaint wooden houses, whilst here and there a tall, armed knight strode by, accompanied by a small body-guard of picked followers.

23

Edwy's cheeks glowed and his eyes sparkled as he gazed on the animated scenes around him. Many were the eager queries he addressed to his brother; queries often answered with an unusual curtness, sometimes not answered at all.

Though Gurth remained somewhat silent, his eyes were busy, and his ears too, though he would fain have shut out from the latter the French words and phrases which assailed them so frequently. No one had recognised him, and he had not met the face of a single friend. Suddenly he pulled up and seized Edwy's bridle-arm sharply.

"Dost see yonder fellow strutting so proudly along?" he exclaimed, at the same time pointing to the narrow roadway which led down to the main gate of the abbey.

The boy glanced in the direction indicated.

"I do," he answered. "Who is it?"

"Gilbert of Tournay, thy enemy and mine," said Gurth; adding, "Our mother will at least have peace from him whilst we are away. Perhaps he hath come hither to crave from the king the gift of her hand in marriage. It would not be the first time that a Norman thief hath done so much."

The Saxon lad spoke angrily and bitterly now, and he looked so long at the retreating, mailed figure, that a man-at-arms touched him lightly on the hand and asked whether he wished to speak to the "noble knight."

Gurth started round and looked the fellow full in the face. "Ay!" replied he sharply, "but not now."

The two lads rode quickly on again. When they

had gone a little distance the elder remarked, "That last sight hath given me my fill of sightseeing for the present. Come, let us seek the house of John the Smith in Eadburga Street, where our mother bade us stay."

In a few moments more they stopped at the door of the worthy craftsman. An apprentice lolled lazily against the doorpost—a sure sign that his master was absent, for John the Smith was well known as a clever and industrious workman, and as a master who allowed no idleness in those who worked for him. At such a time too as the present, when the city was full of soldiers, a trusted smith would have his hands full of work. Gurth enquired of the apprentice whether his master was at home. The youth replied that he was not, and that he would not be at home until noon.

"Then," said Gurth, "is his wife, the good dame Alicia, within?"

"Ay," answered the other slowly, "she is."

Upon this Gurth dismounted, handed the bridle of his pony to the apprentice, and bade him take the somewhat tired steeds to the stables. The youth eyed the two lads for a moment, then did as he was told, and Gurth and Edwy entered the house.

The good-wife of the smith welcomed the lads most cordially. She had been apprised of their coming some days before, and everything was in readiness for their reception.

She and her good-man were Forest bred, and both were in a way connected with the house of Wulf. Alicia's father had been house-carle to Gurth's father

and grandfather, whilst John, son of another house-
carle, had been bound apprentice to a noted smith
of Cinderford.   Having early made a reputation
beyond that of his master, he no sooner found himself
out of his apprenticeship than he married Alicia
and sought wealth and renown in the city.   Both
these had undoubtedly come to him.   His work was
the best along the western border, and it was whispered
amongst the bold youths of the city that the fair
daughter of the smith would have a marriage portion
worthy of the purse of a merchant.   In all city
matters the opinion of the stout smith was one that
received most respectful consideration.

The house of John the Smith, too, was no mean
dwelling-place, and it was not every man—even of
thane's rank—who would have found welcome lodgment there as did Gurth and Edwy.   But the worthy
John and his good-wife still looked upon Gurth as
their natural lord and master.   Their fathers had
served his, they themselves had served the house
of Wulf in their youth, and their friends and relatives
were still its sworn vassals.

Concerning these friends and relatives Alicia had
many questions to ask ; many respectful enquiries too
did she make as to the doings and sayings of the Lady
of the Dean, who, before her marriage into a higher
sphere, had been a companion and playfellow of hers.

Edwy claimed a great deal of her attention ; she
had never seen the lad before, and was liberal in her
praises of his " sweet face and bonny curls."

The good woman had no son of her own, and Edwy
was of that frank, engaging, boyish nature which

appeals so strongly to a sonless mother's heart. He bore her caresses and endearments somewhat shame-facedly, much to the amusement of Gurth.

In this genial happy fashion the morning sped quickly away, and the noon soon came, bringing with it the return of the smith himself. His welcome of the lads was no less warm than that of his wife, but more boisterous and a little less deferential. He was in the forefront of a famous profession and proud of his position.

"I am pleased to see ye both!" he exclaimed, grasping a hand of theirs warmly in each of his own. "And how wags the world with thee? How is the good lady, your mother? and how fare the good folk of the Forest?"

"Well, John," answered Gurth; "and I thank thee for thy greeting. I have little need to ask thee of thy health, thy face speaks well in praise of it; and as to thy affairs, thy good-wife tells me they prosper more than ever."

"I thank God that in that matter her fair words are but simple truth," replied the smith. "Fortune hath been ever kind to me, and this visit of our king is like to advance me more. I will tell thee that I am in good hopes that he will accept a sword at my hands."

"If that be so, I trust thou wilt so far honour thy birthplace as to make it of good Forest steel," said Gurth.

"I will make it of no other!" cried John, bringing his fist down on the table by way of emphasis. "It shall be true Forest blade from the mines of Wulf and from mine own smithy. Moreover, I had proposed, my lord Gurth,—if thou wilt so far honour a vassal of the house—to forge thee thy first full man's sword from the same bar."

"There thou dost honour me!" exclaimed Gurth, springing to his feet, his eyes glistening with pleasure.

"It is what I always hoped to do for thee, as the good-wife knows," said John quietly.

"And I promise thee that, after thou shalt put it in mine hands, I will use no other. A Forest blade should be used to defend the Forest rights."

"Which I promise me it will do, as long as the hand of a Wulf shall wield it," added John. "But come, good dame, have not thy maids prepared the noonday repast?"

"It awaits thee," replied Alicia.

"Then we'll to it, for, by the saints of this sharp Christmastide weather, I'm hungry! And so should our young masters be, too, after their ride. I know the Forest appetite."

"Which appetite I am full eager to show thee again, John," said Gurth laughingly.

"Come, then," cried the host, drawing aside some thick woollen hangings and disclosing a well-spread table, around which the apprentices were already gathered.

The two guests were placed at the right hand of their host at the top, cross-wise placed table, on his left hand being his wife and his daughter Elgiva, the last-named making her appearance for the first time. Gurth greeted her kindly, and courteously presented her to his younger brother.

During the progress of the meal, our host and his guests chattered freely and familiarly upon private concerns of mutual interest, and the rare and more enthralling topic, the visit of the king.   On this matter the lads had many questions to ask, and the good smith, well acquainted with all that went on, was only too pleased to give them every information. The good-wife Alicia looked after the creature comfort of the apprentices with a motherly interest, and the latter for some time bent all their energies to eating and drinking, with just a glance at the fair daughter of the house and the two noble guests by way of relaxation.

As soon, however, as the claims of their appetites became less pressing, their tongues began to wag freely.   There was just a round dozen of them, and on all subjects except three, there was, as a rule, a round dozen of more or less contrary opinions.   The three subjects upon which they were all agreed were : First, that John the Smith was anything but an easy master to serve.   Second, that the Dame Alicia was a good, motherly soul, who deserved to have a son, for she looked after other mothers' sons so well. The third subject may well be divided into three parts.   It concerned the smith's daughter, and the parts were as follows :—Firstly, she was the most winsome lassie 'neath the blue dome of heaven ; secondly, the apprentice—that is, the *good* apprentice —often wooed and won his master's daughter, if he had one ; thirdly, each apprentice considered himself the appointed youth for this interesting romance.

Many a swollen nose, many a cracked skull, many a blackened eye had the smith's fair daughter helped to doctor, little suspecting that she herself was the innocent cause of the wounds and bruises.

And now, no doubt, many of our young readers are anxious to know what the young lady herself was like. We will satisfy their natural curiosity.

Elgiva—for so the young lady was called—had just entered her seventeenth year. She was fair, blue-eyed, tall; her hair was flaxen and wavy; her face decidedly pretty, and also decidedly roguish and mischievous. The quiet humour lurking in her merry eyes and in the dimpled corners of her mouth had kept many a youthful tongue silent, and many a bashful young apprentice in the background; they were afraid to speak or act, lest they should be made to appear foolish and ridiculous.

To say she ruled the household was only to speak the bare truth. Her father idolised her, her mother loved her as only a fond mother can love an only child, whilst every apprentice was her devoted slave. Elgiva was, however, no tyrant; she delighted not to be waited upon, but to wait upon others. Many a poor house-wife, many a sick child, knew her as their best friend. So the apprentices of John the Smith, each and all, loved his only daughter and quarrelled and fought over her in right good fashion.

To-day they forgot their rivalry, forgot to watch each other, and regarded only the young thane of the house of Wulf. Why came he from his Forest home at Yuletide? Why lodged he in the house of the smith? Did he love their young mistress, or did he

covet only her father's wealth ? These were troublesome questions, and each sinewy youth made it his
business to trouble greatly about them.

They might well, however, have spared all their little
heart-burnings and questionings. The son of Wulf
came not to woo the fair daughter of the smith ; other
and weightier reasons brought him from home at
Yuletide. Indeed, so engrossed was he by these
reasons that he had not given one thought to Elgiva
since he had presented his brother to her.

On the other hand, Edwy, neglected by his brother
and the smith, spent much of his time in gazing at
the young girl. The merry sparkle in her eyes
proclaimed her to be quite the equal of his own
sister at a romp, and he heartily wished himself at her
side. Edwy was still of an age when a merry girl
is looked upon as a desirable playmate, whilst Gurth,
just springing into manhood, had ceased to think of
them as playmates, and had not yet begun to think
of them as helpmates. Therefore did the apprentices
of John the Smith trouble their minds unnecessarily.

Dinner, protracted longer than usual, came to an
end at length, and each one set about his or her
particular duty or pleasure. Edwy found himself
where he had wished to be—namely, at Elgiva's side,
engaged in a sprightly conversation. Gurth and the
smith were inspecting the forge and workshop of the
latter, whither, too, the apprentices had returned
to work. Dame Alicia was about her household
duties. Thus engaged, we will leave them now until
the time of sunset.

CHAPTER III.

DURING the afternoon Gurth had made the smith fully acquainted with the object of his visit, and had received from him much sound and serviceable advice.

The young thane was particularly anxious to get some knowledge of the real temper and disposition of the king, for much as he depended upon the justice and chivalry of his cause, yet he desired to place everything in as effective a light as possible. Gurth had his own ideas of what a king should be, but rumour in the western shires credited the Conqueror with many unkingly attributes. To most minds he was a harsh, unscrupulous tyrant, a hater and oppressor of the Saxon, and chiefly bent upon enriching himself and rewarding rascally followers.

Much of this Gurth disbelieved, and some of it the smith swore to be untrue.

" Stark man he is, I grant thee, to them that withstand him ; strong is he in will and in arm ; yet is his will not always directed to work evil, nor his arm to bruise and slay. I would trust a good cause to his judgment rather than to that of any other man in England ! There, my lord, is my opinion," said John.

" But what if he hath promised aught to any man ? " asked Gurth. " And how stands this master-thief, Gilbert of Tournay, with him ? "

" Ha ! there," answered the smith, " thou hast cause for much disquiet. He will not break his word without good reason, and I fear the knight stands well in the king's graces."

" He is liar and nithing ! " cried Gurth angrily.

" Then prove him that, and thyself true man, and I know in what quarter the king's favour will lie," said the smith.

" The point is," replied Gurth, " whether the king be concerned in this fellow's knaveries. If so, it will hardly please the master-knave to hear his servant proclaimed a rogue."

" On that point I cannot help thee," said John.

The smith and the young thane then separated, and shortly afterwards the latter went forth into the city and walked in the direction of the river. He paced up and down the high banks, and watched the swollen, muddy stream as it swept on in the direction of his own home. He lifted his eyes to the western horizon, which glowed luridly with the deep red of the winter sunset. The same red light, he knew, dyed the turrets and gables of his Forest home. His thoughts flew thither instantly. How fared his lady-mother, the angel and idol of his warm, youthful heart ? What news should he carry back to her ? Would they be glad or sorry ? Would tears of joy or tears of pain spring to his mother's eyes when next they lighted on him ?

These and many other questions the lad asked

himself as he gazed over the low, rich meadows towards the dark hills which studded the Forest. His mood had changed considerably since he entered the city in the fresh early morning. Young, brave, hopeful, he was inexperienced in the ways of kings, and courts, and cities. He had but little skill in, and no taste for, intrigue. He could meet a foe boldly, and strike hard; but he gathered from the shrewd, worldly remarks of the smith, that something more than a stout heart, a truthful tongue, and a fearless eye was necessary to fight the crooked ways of knavish foes. Though not dispirited, he was grown less sanguine, and his first simple, manly scheme for appealing to the king seemed to have grown childish.

Pondering ways and means of action, he stood by the Severn until the last red rays of the sun were vanquished by the strong, silvern beams of the moon. Then he turned citywards, entered the gates again, and strode slowly and thoughtfully up the Westgate Street. Instead of proceeding at once to the house of the smith he wended his way towards the abbey, curiosity prompting him to a closer survey of the walls which he must soon enter in order to appeal to the royal guest within.

A beautiful sight was not lost upon Gurth, bred as he had been in the arms of untamed nature and the wild solitudes of the Forest. He stood in the shadow of a buttress near a sharp angle of the wall, and gazed with a feeling of pride upon the scene before him,—the folk of the western shire were truly proud of their ancient capital city.

The moonlight streamed down on pinnacle, tower, and turret, casting long shadows on the snow-strewn roof, and flashing from the crystal icicles which hung pendant from the overhanging stonework and tracery. From within the walls came mingled sounds of voices and the ring and clang of arms and armour, and from the large, mullioned casements flared the red light of torches. The main gate of the abbey, which was only a few yards distant, stood wide open, and knight and soldier, monk and tradesman passed and repassed its portals.

Gurth drew a little nearer, and as he did so two tall figures came down the narrow roadway from the street. He halted, and his blood warmed as he observed the easy, insolent air with which they approached. He had noticed that but few Saxons of the city held themselves so proudly. As the two came on he saw that one was in full armour, whilst the other, and apparently younger one, was lightly armed and foppishly dressed.

The sound of their voices reached him, and Gurth felt his grip instinctively tighten upon the handle of the light hunting-spear he carried ; his breath, too, came quick and hard.

"Shall I then meet thee morn and night?" he muttered. The armed man was the arch-enemy of his house—Gilbert of Tournay.

They reached the gate, and halted. The knight Gilbert addressed some question to his companion, and the latter, replying with some laughing remark, turned upon his heel and walked rapidly back towards the street.

3

The young thane caught the last few words of this remark, and they immediately riveted his attention upon the speaker. The words were : "Rather is it to steal a kiss from the lips of a pretty Saxon wench." They cut Gurth like the lash of a whip. He knew what they meant, and he remembered a similar coarse remark which Gilbert of Tournay had once made concerning his own mother.

He had vowed to avenge that insult, and he determined now that the young Norman should molest no Saxon maid that night if he could prevent it. He followed him, a fierce anger burning at his heart.

Presently the Norman slackened his pace ; then stopped. Gurth did so too.

"So thy victim is already chosen," he muttered betwixt his firm-set teeth. "The less distance then shall I have to track thee."

He leant on his spear and waited. The minutes flew by, and the young Norman got impatient; but Gurth never stirred. He watched him like a lynx, striving to plainly distinguish his features in the moonlight. This he found impossible to do, but he comforted himself with the thought that he should scan them at closer quarters before long. The house they were both watching was almost within the precincts of the abbey.

At last the door opened, and a hooded, girlish figure stepped forth into the moonlight. The Norman came from his hiding-place and stole after it ; Gurth followed him. The girl had not gone many yards before she perceived that she was followed. She stopped suddenly in her walk. After a moment's hesitation

she turned back in the pathway and took a narrower
but shorter one leading into the Westgate Street.

Gurth smiled grimly. " Yon Norman," he muttered,
" will find a score or so of stout Saxon youths ready
to crack his skull, if he meddle with the maiden in
the main thoroughfare."

The Norman apparently thought the same, for he
considerably quickened his pace, and, unless the
girl took to running, bade fair to intercept her in
the darkest and narrowest part of the path. Gurth
followed as doggedly as Fate. The Norman gained,
stride by stride ; and at length the girl, after casting
repeated glances behind her, gave up the race as hopeless, and leant, panting and breathless, against the side
of a small house in the sharp angle of the pathway.

The Norman laughed softly ; she could not have
stopped in a better place. A minute more and he
was beside her.

The girl stood with tightened lips, and for a moment
looked at him proudly and defiantly. Then she spoke.
" Why do you follow me, sir ? "

The Norman made a mock courtesy, and replied :
" My pretty one, would you ask why life follows the
sun ?—or rather why my poor lunatic fancy should
follow its glorious moon ? "

The girl made no answer.

" You are silent, my pretty damsel ! "

" I have nothing to say to you, except that it is
not manly to stop a defenceless girl."

" Be not so harsh," said the fellow lispingly. " I
will be your knight—by my soul ! you are worthy one
—and will escort you whither you are going, asking

no favour higher than a kiss from those pretty lips. Believe me, it was to protect so beautiful a maiden that I left my friends and turned back to wait for you."

Again the girl made no answer, only tapped her foot impatiently.

The young Norman sighed affectedly and continued his chatter.

"Ah! sweet one," said he, "those pretty lips are pale and pressed all out of shape. Come, just one kiss will bring the rich colour back again, and charm them into the form of Cupid's bow."

He made a step forward, reaching out his left arm as if to encircle her waist. It never so much as touched the hem of her cloak. There was the sound of a quick "swish" in the air, then a resounding "crack," and the Norman sprang back with an oath. English ash had met Norman bone; the result, the Norman bone in the wrist had cracked like a dry twig!

Quickly following the blow there came the apparition which had dealt it. Its arm immediately and vigorously wound itself round the waist of the trembling girl. Moreover, there was no demur; but instead, a quick cry of joy and a whispered exclamation, "Gurth!" And this happy exclamation came from the lips of Elgiva, the bonny daughter of John the Smith!

All this had taken place in an instant, and in an instant too the Norman recovered his self-possession. His right hand was uninjured. He drew his dagger, and with a cry of pain and rage sprang at Gurth.

The Saxon lad, however, was as quick as his assailant. There was another ominous "swish," and the dagger went spinning into the air.

"*Diable!*" yelled the baffled fellow, wringing his hand.

Gurth gave a quiet laugh, and, striding forward, turned his foe's face to the light of the moon. He scanned it intently.

"I shall know thee again," he said.

"I shall know thee, too, thou varlet!" hissed the other. His right hand was only bruised, and he attempted to draw his sword. Gurth sent him sprawling into the snow.

"Thou shalt hang for this at thy master's door," cried the Norman, staggering to his feet.

"That will be before the king's palace, then," answered Gurth, "for I own service to no other man."

"Thou shalt hang at mine, thou Saxon knave!"

"The Norman cur shall hardly hang the Saxon Wulf!"

"Ah! Wulf, sayest thou?"

"Ay! Thou canst tell thy brother cur—him of Tournay—that thou hast felt the Wulf's fangs. They shall tug at his throat before long."

Without another word Gurth turned on his heel and walked away. The Norman watched his retreating figure, then picked up his dagger, and went towards the abbey.

"So this is the stripling of whom Gilbert spake. His house shall make a fire to thaw a frosty night before this winter is out," he muttered.

Gurth and his charge walked on rapidly and in silence. They crossed the Westgate Street. Then Elgiva stopped.

"I cannot walk so quickly," she said.

"Forgive my thoughtlessness!" cried Gurth sorrowfully. "My blood is heated, and I marked not the pace at which I was going."

He gave her his hand, and they went slowly on.

"I have not thanked thee yet for my deliverance," said Elgiva timidly.

"But I have thanked myself in my good fortune," answered Gurth, with a smile. "Why didst thou go forth alone? Would none of the 'prentice-lads accompany thee? They are stout fellows and well able to keep meddling rascals at a distance."

Elgiva blushed, and her hand trembled in Gurth's. "I cannot have them, they would quarrel with every Norman who looked at me," she said hurriedly; "and thou knowest what yon fellow said of hanging at their master's door."

Gurth glanced at her laughingly. He saw the blush.

"I know he spake of hanging *me*," he answered merrily. "Hast thou no care for *my* life?"

"Yes, yes ; but—but, I would rather thou didst me the service. I mean—I mean, he cannot hang thee ; thou art of noble birth."

Poor Elgiva blushed rosily. red this time, and in her confusion loosed her hold on Gurth's hand.

He blushed too, and looked intently at the point of his spear. He took her hand again. "I would rather, too, that I did thee this service. 'Tis a duty I owe thine house."

"Yes, that is it," cried Elgiva, quickening her pace to an alarming rate. "We are vassals still of the house of Wulf, and it seems meet that its lord should shield us."

Gurth was now in no mood for hurry. Eadburga Street was close at hand. Soon the two were walking more slowly than ever.

Elgiva spoke again. "Thou wilt not tell my father what has happened?"

"Not if thou wilt promise me to go forth no more alone."

"I will ask my father to accompany me."

"And if he cannot come?"

"I do not know."

"Thou wilt stay at home?"

"I cannot always. There are sick ones to visit."

"While I am here, wilt thou make me thy companion on these errands of mercy?"

"I cannot do so. I will take some apprentice-lads whom my father shall choose."

"Thou shalt do that after I'm gone. Thou hast shown me that it is my duty to protect the vassals of mine house; and there is none worthier of that protection than thou art," added the young thane warmly.

The blood tingled in the girl's cheeks as she murmured a few shy words of thanks.

Gurth's cheeks were glowing too. They reached the door; their hands were still clasped. They looked each into the other's face. Elgiva's eyes were moist; and there was a little lump in Gurth's throat. He looked at her lips; they were full of colour now and trembling. He thought of the Norman's words. Elgiva thought of them too, and her heart throbbed, almost painfully. Gurth bent his head, then raised her fingers to his lips. A little sob escaped the girl as they entered the house.

CHAPTER IV.

IN WHICH GURTH MEETS THE KING.

ONE result of Gurth's evening adventure was a night of broken and fitful slumber ; an actual encounter with one of his foes had stirred his blood and fired his spirits, and he burned now to grasp the smith's sword and head an onslaught upon them all. He had never greatly desired a peaceful settlement of the feud ; he desired it less than ever now. It was well that he sojourned at present under the roof of the shrewd and worldly-wise smith ; had the thane Orcar been his host, some jointly-planned deed of daring might have given matters an ugly, perhaps fatal turn. Many such wild plans coursed through his brain.

Long before day dawned, the male portion of the smith's household was astir. There was much to be done ; so, whilst the wintry sky still throbbed in the clear starlight, the forges roared, the anvils clanged, and the bright steel flashed in the fire and torchlight. The sounds came dully to the ears of Gurth ; they rang in tune with his warlike thoughts, and he arose from his pallet, dressed, and went forth into the frosty, starlit morning.

He bent his steps towards the smithy, pushed open the great oaken wicket, and entered.

At the nearest anvil, clad in leathern tunic and

apron, his great arms bared to the shoulder, stood the
doughty John. With a short-hafted but weighty
hammer, he rained vigorous and resounding blows
upon a short piece of glowing steel which a young
apprentice held in a pair of pincers. Near to him two
other smiths were similarly engaged upon a long
bar. Scattered around in little groups were others
who hammered, or burnished, or polished. One
sturdy apprentice plied the bellows handle with might
and main. The smoke wreathed and rolled in snaky
clouds amongst the rafters ; the fires roared, the
anvils rang, the sparks flew, the water hissed and
steamed, the torches smoked and flared ; everywhere
was din and clangour, smoke and fire. Vulcan himself could not have made more heat and noise. Gurth,
chilled as he was with a night of restless tossing and
a half-sleepy excursion into the biting, morning air,
felt his whole frame glow as he watched them.

> "When the dawn is rung in with the smithy's din
>   There's a fight to lose—and a fight to win ! "

sang a yellow-haired apprentice-lad as he held the edge
of a ponderous axe upon the flying grinding-wheel.

Gurth started ; the words were an echo of his own
thoughts.

The smith looked up and bade him a cheery " good-
morning ! " A moment later he bellowed : " There
is something in yon corner to please thine eye ! "
He paused just long enough in his hammering to
indicate a distant corner of the building, and then
the din rang out again.

Gurth threaded his way amongst the workmen

in the direction in which the smith's hammer had pointed, and found himself by the side of a venerable artificer—indeed, none other than the famous Leofric, the most renowned engraver of devices in steel which the whole of the western and midland shires possessed.

Gurth had heard of the marvellous cunning of Leofric in his work, but he had never before met him face to face.

The engraver looked up as the newcomer halted near him, and subjected him to a not too friendly scrutiny. At the unmistakable Saxon appearance of the young thane, however, his features relaxed into something like a smile: during the past few days he had had more than enough of the masterful airs and remarks of the young Norman bloods who had come in the train of the king. It was upon the blade of the king's sword that he was now working, and he wrought with a sullen determination to make the blade worthy the scabbard of the proudest king in Christendom, and worthy also of the skill and cunning of a Saxon graver.

He paused for a while in his work and looked at Gurth, watching the face of the latter as he gazed with admiration upon the steel lying on the bench before him.

Neither spoke, but there was a look of pleasure on the old fellow's face as he bent again to his task. The ends of his long white beard trailed on his work, and the steel curled in long, thin strips before the keen edge of the graver's tool, guided as it was with un- erring force and precision by the long, nervous fingers

and quick grey eye of Leofric. The design, of crowns
and lions, dragons and serpents, and warlike mottoes
in quaint Saxon characters, was nearly completed
ere Gurth appeared.

Soon came the melting-pot and the gold, and the
young thane saw the devices blazoned forth in
glittering yellow lines. His heart throbbed as the
whole thing grew before his eyes.

The time flew on ; an hour had passed. Then
suddenly clang and clamour ceased, the whirr and
hiss stopped, and master, men, and apprentices prepared to respond to the call to the morning meal.
The smith came to see the progress of the work, and
he rubbed his hands with glee as he beheld it.

" What thinkest thou of that, my lord ? " cried he
to Gurth.

" It is worthy the hand of Odin himself! " answered
the youth enthusiastically.

"Thou art right. And, mark me, it shall teach
the tongues and necks of the slanderers of our Saxon
handicraft a lesson. It is right well and truly wrought,
and proud am I to have forged the steel for the good
Leofric's hand."

"Thy steel, Sir Smith, is worthy any man's chisel,"
replied Leofric gravely; " I have never put point to
harder or truer metal."

" Then should the king be satisfied," said Gurth,
with an envious sigh ; and, with one more lingering
look at the glittering object, he turned towards the
open wicket through which workman and apprentice
had clamorously passed some minutes before. John
and Leofric followed.

The morning meal was taken in haste, and with less than the usual amount of clamour. Indeed, with the exception of Edwy and one or two of the younger and more heedless apprentices, all seemed more or less preoccupied. Gurth's mind was filled with many wonderings and vague schemes, and a presentiment of immediate happenings of great import troubled him. He determined to set out with his brother and seek relaxation by another ramble through the streets of the city. He longed, too, for another glance at the face of the familiar river.

Immediately after breakfast he set forth, and in a quarter of an hour stood by the water's side. There was a keen north-east wind blowing, and this and the ruddy-tinged December sun had effectually cleared the morning mists from the damp, low-lying, river meadows. Both lads felt cheered and inspirited, and, at the suggestion of Edwy, strode off to watch a game of hockey, at that moment in full swing on one of the frozen meadow ponds.

The players were youthful, and withal noisy. Suddenly the noise increased to a marked extent; there was a quick rush to one corner of the pond, a great brandishing of sticks, a confused babel of shouts and angry exclamations, then clear, shrill cries of " To the river ! " " Duck him ! " and the whole body ran clamorously riverwards, hustling in their midst a showily-dressed boy who screamed and struggled against them in vain. Gurth started towards them with a quick run, but they were before him, and with yells of anger and derision hurled the hapless youngster down the steep, snow-covered banks, crashing through the withered reeds into the yellow, muddy, icy river. Our young thane was just in time to see him rise, gasping and voiceless, from his unwelcome bath. Hardly slackening his pace, he slid down the bank, swam out to the unlucky victim, and dragged him ashore ere he could sink again. This done, he turned quickly upon the now silent crowd of adversaries, and demanded what they meant by all turning upon one lad.

"He is Norman!" blurted out one rosy, yellow-haired urchin.

"He called us ugly names, and laughed at our game," added another ; and the babel began again. The chorus of it all was : "He is Norman ! proud ! insolent ! To the river with the saucy dog !"

"Ye are a pack of cowards !" said Gurth warmly. "Could not one of ye come forward and fight him, man to man ? I'm ashamed of ye ; the Norman hath better pluck, and I have a mind to trounce ye all for your lack of Saxon fair play. And as for you," added he, turning to the shivering, dripping page (for such his dress betokened him to be), "it would become you to learn good manners, and to keep a humbler tongue in your head."

"I would teach thee better manners, Sir Saxon, than to talk to me of humility towards yon swine, were it not that thou hast rendered me good service," responded the youth, as hotly and with as much dignity as his loudly chattering teeth permitted him. "And as for ye," cried he, turning to his foes, "if there be a whole skin left among ye by vesper time, my name is not Geoffrey de Tarbeux." So saying he stalked loftily away, followed by threats, challenges, and taunts, which he was sarcastically invited to scatter broadcast amongst his Norman friends.

After a few moments spent in pacifying and lecturing the hotheaded English youngsters, Gurth, prompted by a sudden thought, turned and hastily followed in the wake of the Norman boy. The latter had advanced but a little way citywards, and to Gurth his steps appeared to grow perceptibly shorter and slower. A short, quick run and he was at his side. He found his conjecture was only too true. Under the biting influence of the keen north-east wind it was freezing sharply. Young de Tarbeux's sodden clothes were stiffening round his limbs, and these were already almost benumbed inside their icy and clammy covering. A few more feeble strides and he must have fallen. Without a word, Gurth seized one arm, Edwy another, and between them they dragged the half-frozen youngster along at a brisk pace. Circulation was soon partially restored, but Gurth, catching sight of a serf's cottage in an angle of the meadow, made off at once towards it, for he deemed that the sooner the boy found warmth and shelter the better it would be for him. They gained instant admission, and in a short time the unlucky· one lay before the blazing fire of turf, snugly wrapped in a sheepskin, and moodily sipping a horn of warm mead, his clothes spread on a rude bench near him.

After extracting a promise from the rough but kindly "huswife" that she would carefully tend her charge for a few hours, the two young Saxons left

him and wended their way back towards the city.
Gurth was chilled and benumbed himself, and, although
he had taken advantage of his brief stay in the
shepherd's hut to partially dry himself, still, he felt
that the sooner he reached the smith's house the better
for his comfort.

On reaching Eadburga Street, however, our young
Saxons saw that something unusual was astir ; horses,
servitors, and pages thronged the roadway, and gaping
youths and men crowded and crushed in every doorway and under every arch. Having no servitors to
run before them and cry " Make way ! " they found
progress a slow and difficult matter, especially as the
crowd, both of followers and loiterers, increased as
they neared the smith's house. Indeed, had it not been
for a timely meeting with an apprentice, who loudly
proclaimed their degree and place of lodgment, it is
probable that they would have reached their destination
only when the cavalcade moved onward from it.
Very few moments amongst the jostling throng sufficed
to inform Gurth that the cause of all was no less a
matter than a visit of the king to the smithy of his
friend John.

The young lads' pulses quickened as they realised
this. Gurth saw an opportunity of seeing and studying
the king without tremor or embarrassment, an advantage too important and too valuable to be lost.
He therefore elbowed his way more lustily than ever
through the throng, earning by this proceeding many a
muttered curse from the Norman henchmen. These,
however, he wisely let pass unheeded, and presently
found himself in the spacious hall of the smith's house,

panting and heated, his damp clothes clinging clammily to his warm limbs.

He hastily thanked the young apprentice who had so opportunely come to his assistance, and then hurried away to don the only change of clothing he had with him—viz., those which he had provided for his audience with the king. This was soon accomplished, and in a few moments Gurth and Edwy had ensconced themselves in a darkened corner of the smithy, but in such a position that they could easily see the king as he stood near the forge examining a number of weapons of the smith's construction. A score or so of his nobles stood around him in holiday attire, and the smith and Leofric the graver stood immediately at his side to answer his questions concerning their work.

As the lads entered, William, the only one of the company clad in complete armour, stood, poising in his hand a tremendous battle-axe. His huge frame being by this action stretched to the uttermost, and his kindling eye dwelling critically on the weapon extended before him, Gurth was fain to own that he looked kingly indeed ; the thought gave him pleasure, for he saw cause to hope that such a king would not be trifled with by any follower, however powerful.

Whilst standing thus, the king spoke, and his voice was robust and ringing.

" What say ye, my lords," cried he, speaking in French, " is it not well wrought and worthy ? " Then, turning to the smith, he added in Saxon, " And what arm is it that shall wield this gleaming mass of steel ? "

"A good Saxon servant of my lord king," replied the smith.

Several of the nobles murmured in disapprobation at this, and William turned sharply with a "Ha! Sir Smith, thou givest my subjects brave weapons!"

"But," quickly answered the ready John, "I give their king a braver." So saying, he stooped and lifted a large rolled wolfskin near him. He unrolled it, and there lay glittering and glinting in the ruddy firelight a truly enormous axe, hafted with stoutest ash and bound with three golden bands. The light tinged its edge with the hue of blood. A cry of astonishment burst from the group; even William himself uttered a loud exclamation and bent eagerly forward.

"There!" cried the smith exultingly, turning it handle-wise to the king, "there lies a wolf-tooth that in a kingly hand shall bite the brain of the doughtiest in Christendom or heathendom. Will my lord king accept it at my hands?"

"Accept it!" cried William, seizing it and brandishing it aloft as though it were a toy, to the wonderment of all. "Kneel thee, Sir Smith. By death! if to combat the king's enemies be worthy of reward, then thou art worthy of much, for thy good right arm hath fashioned the death of thousands. Knight thou art worthy to be, smith or no smith, and knight thou shalt be, or I am no king. Rise, Sir John! with thine own made weapon I knight thee."

Suiting action to the word, the king let the axe fall flat and lightly on the smith's shoulder.

Sir John rose to his feet, his face flushing with pride and pleasure. In an instant, however, he bent

4

the knee again, seized the king's mailed hand and kissed it reverently.

"My lord king," said he, "you have honoured my craft and me; henceforth my skill, arm, and heart are yours!"

There was a generous enthusiasm in the old smith's manner which struck the king. He raised him up and remarked quietly:

"Sir Smith, thy heart will be as true as thy steel."

By this time the surrounding nobles had recovered from their consternation, and disgust and contempt hovered on many a face. William seemed to divine something of this, for he turned sharply towards them and exclaimed:

"Ha! my lords, methinks this is ill-pleasing to some of you. If the morsel be bitter to your palates, I counsel ye not to hesitate to bolt it whole. Swallow it ye must, and mayhap over-much chewing may be bad for your stomachs."

This last sentence was accompanied by a smile so full of sinister meaning that the train made all haste to compose their countenances. Seeing this the king went on:

"There was once a king ruled these realms, and all men joined in calling him the 'Wise and Great.' He fought well and hardily, my lords, against a doughty foe. So have I. When settled in his kingdom he rewarded those who had helped him to win it. Then he turned to those who could help him to enrich it—to his handicraftsmen and scholars, and he rewarded them and made them thanes and

knights. I love the memory of that king, so ye are like ere long to see nobles among ye who never donned helm or hauberk."

Without waiting to see the effect of his words, William turned to the smith, and said it would pleasure him greatly to see some further proofs of his wonderful skill and craft.

Sir John, nothing loth, showed him many a keen and deadly dagger, many a sharp and weighted spear, many a straight and well-trimmed arrow ; and the king expressed himself as mightily pleased with all.

During this inspection they had wandered from point to point in the smithy, and now stood at the bench on which Leofric the graver was wont to work. On it lay the sword intended for the king, and also the half-finished, but exactly similar, blade intended for Gurth. The latter, who during all this time had remained in his corner an excited and delighted spectator, now leaned eagerly forward to catch what the king might say.

Sir John handed the sword to the king, and William examined it long and attentively. He tried the temper of its blade, its balance, its weight ; he scrutinised most carefully its quaint designs and inlaid work ; then he laid it on the bench again with something very like a sigh.

" Sir Smith," said he, "thou hast made me almost forget yon goodly axe. What may be the meaning of these characters and designs ? "

" So please you, my king," replied the smith, "they are to illustrate and tell stories of our greatest kings' and warriors' deeds. But my worthy fellow-craftsman, the aged Leofric, who wrought them, can better tell thee of them than can I."

The king turned to Leofric, and without speaking, scanned for a moment the quiet countenance of the venerable Saxon. Then he quietly remarked: " I did not know that my kingdom possessed such cunning workmen. I would like to hear the stories of this blade, but it shall not be now; thou shalt recount them in my hall, so that all my court may hear, and learn what a brave people it is God has put into their hands for rule and guidance. We hold high court to-night, Master Graver, and it would be the better for thy presence, and for thine, too, Sir John; there will be seats for ye both, and room for a Saxon sword."

The smith and the graver bowed, and the latter, who had hitherto not spoken, addressed the king.

" My lord," said he, " thou hast spoken words to-day in praise of handicraft that had been deemed gracious from the lips of good King Alfred, whom thou hast so well and wisely extolled. I had not thought to hear such from thee. This sword was wrought for thee, and thou wilt spare grey hairs when I tell thee of my share in the work. What I did, I did from no love of thee, but from a pride in our Saxon craft. I tell thee this because now I would pray forgiveness for my unkindly thoughts. Thou art kingly enough to be worthy the best work, and I make thee free offer of all that is left my old hands to do."

Leofric spoke simply and with rough, blunt Saxon

dignity. William proved himself kingly enough to forget all that might have ruffled his kingship.

"Thou too, I see," said he, "art honest. Well, I thank thee for a princely gift. Thou hast given me of thy best. Thou shalt find that William, Norman or no Norman, is thy king, and no niggard. Sir Smith, I owe thee great thanks again. Thou art making me deeply thy debtor. Thou, too, shalt find that thy king can give a kingly reward."

He turned to his train.

"Nobles," exclaimed he, "we have seen enow. We will be gone."

He then turned again to Sir John and Leofric.

"Bring the goodly weapons ye have wrought for us to the abbey to-night; we will receive them at your hands in the presence of all."

With a smile to the Saxons around him, William turned to the smithy door and departed. His train followed, but their countenances were hardly as pleasant as their king's.

He left, however, pleasanter ones behind him, and great was the joy upon the faces of the smith, the graver, and our two young heroes as they turned into the house to tell the good Dame Alicia ("Dame" now in right good earnest) the glorious news.

CHAPTER V.

A T the smith's house the few remaining hours
of the short winter day were spent in the bustle
of the great preparation. The worthy Sir John and
his good Dame busied themselves right heartily, for
they had quickly decided that both men and women,
maids and apprentices, should feast right royally and
loyally for the sake of the king and their much-
honoured master. On the other hand, men and apprentices bestirred and bedecked themselves, each, and
every one alike determined to form part of a fit and
goodly retinue worthy of the new knight. Elgiva
for once did nothing ; she spent her time in pleasant
musings and in smiling happily at the bustling
endeavours of both parties. Gurth spent his time
in the real and necessary preparations for Sir John's
appearance in the king's court in the chapter-room
of the venerable abbey. Leofric was at his bench
putting finishing touches to the king's sword.

Sunset brought cessation from labour and also the
hour at which the two craftsmen were to appear
in the presence of their king. Torches were lit, Sir
John donned his bravest attire, which consisted
mainly of garments made of the softest leather, a
grey cloak of Saxon woollen cloth, spun by his own

58

good Dame, and a wolfskin cap. His sole weapon was a short dagger. Leofric wore the holiday attire of a wealthy craftsman. The whole household stood in the hall ; even the cook and her maids and scullions left, for a moment, the kitchen and its cares behind them, and came to gaze upon their transformed master. They, moreover, brought with them the odours, rich and manifold, of the great repast upon which their energies had now for some time been expended.

The greatest preparations come to an end, and Sir John was at length ready to start. At the last moment, however, he decided to go without his admiring retinue of enthusiastic followers. Such a decision was a disappointment to himself as well as to his men. He had, however, seen that his new dignity was ill-pleasing to the Normans, and, although he cared not one jot for their love or their hatred, yet he wisely forbore to stir up unnecessary strife. He took with him two stout and brawny men, one to act as torch-bearer, the other to carry the king's axe. To Leofric he apportioned a like number, one of whom bore the king's sword. Having promised Gurth to mention him and his errand to the king if opportunity occurred, he wished his servants a hearty enjoyment of the feast, and departed.

We will not follow him, but stay with our young hero, Gurth, who, as he watched the burly smith's form disappear through the doorway, wondered anxiously as to what the night might bring forth.

He sat at the head of the board and assisted the Dame Alicia in the ruling of the feast ; it was a duty which he had often shared in the great castle of

the Dean. At his lead the company toasted their
master, their mistress, the fair Elgiva, and the king.
He smiled proudly when the hostess, taking a horn
of mead from a servitor, raised it to her lips, and
called on all to drink love, health, and honour to
the young thane Wulf, to whom and to whose brave
house they, with their master, owed fealty and service.

The feast went on with a gusto that only a Saxon
feast could acquire. The eating and drinking were
prodigious, the capacities of the feasters inexhaustible.
At the expiration of an hour the two ladies left the
hall. Edwy accompanied them, and Gurth was left
in solitary dignity. His thoughts soon began to
wander. In spirit he was at home. Then he was
at the abbey. He saw the king sitting in state,
the axe and sword before him. Leofric was relating
the deeds of the Saxon heroes and gods. William
listened attentively. Now and then the great company
applauded, but it was when the deeds of Odin and
Balder, and the old heroes of northern mythology
were sung. They, too, came from the north, and
these gods and heroes were in part their own. There
was silence when the deeds of Alfred, of Athelstane,
were recited; only the king maintained an attitude
of pleased attention.

Gurth felt he could love his king. He saw him
fearless, anxious to do right by all his subjects,
anxious for the weal of England, and ruthless and
terrible to his foes. He saw not the sinister side of
the Conqueror's character.

Heedless of his abstraction, the clamour of the
feast went on around him. He heard all dimly, the

confused hubbub of conversation, the voice of the story-teller, the twang of the harp, and the melody of the song it accompanied ; he was faintly conscious of a youthful voice warbling of

" Lightsome lasses lilting strains of love."

Suddenly, however, he recovered his senses with a start. One of the smiths, a fellow who hailed from the Forest, more than half-drunken from deep pota-tions of mead, was roaring forth from a pair of lungs as tough as his own bellows the song of " The House of Wulf."

In an instant Gurth was on his feet too, his hands tightly gripping the edges of the table. In a chant of swinging rhythm the song rolled out :—

" Hist ! the wolf's wail on the wind's wings is stealing,
　　See ! in the moon's beam,
　　Fangs flash, red eyes gleam !
'Ware ! 'ware ! All around you the dread howls are pealing.

" Ho ! sons of the wolf, tame sheep fatten yonder ;
　　Sleek wethers, proud rams,
　　And tenderest lambs ;
Ever dreaming they hear our blood-howl in the thunder,
In each flash of Thor's hammer, the gleam of our flesh-tooth !

" The glowworm and will-o'-the-wisp are our eyes ;
They hear our swift tread in each stir of the wood-growth.
So, sons of the wolf, to the sheep-hunt arise !
Spoil for wife, son, and daughter,
Ye shall win from the slaughter,
List ! list ! how each nithing sheep tremblingly cries.
Hist ! the wolf's wail on the wind's wings is stealing.
　　See ! in the moon's beam,
　　Fangs flash, red eyes gleam !
'Ware ! 'ware ! all around you the blood-howls are pealing ! "

And the blood-howl pealed out at the instant when
the singer ceased.   The whole company leaped to
their feet, and the dreaded war-cry of the Wolf shook
the rafters like the blast of a fierce gale.   Again and
again it rang out; knives flashed from their sheaths,
and glittering eyes were turned upon Gurth, who
stood trembling with passion and emotion at the
head of the table.   His eyes glittered as ominously
as any that were bent upon him.   His mother's spirit
for the moment lay crushed in his heart; nothing
was betokened in his lithe, strained figure save the
bloody savagery of his fierce Forest ancestors.   The
men for a moment gazed upon him, silent, fascinated.
Then he took his purse from his girdle, and hurled it
excitedly down the table, striking the singer full in
his brawny chest.

"A Wulf!"   "A Wulf!"   "A Wulf!" again
rang frantically out.   Men clashed their glittering
knives upon the broad blades of their neighbours' in
wild enthusiasm.

At that moment the curtains over the doorway
were drawn hastily aside, and the smith entered, a
Norman, of apparently high rank, following closely
at his heels.   They surveyed the scene with un-
disguised consternation.

At the sight of drawn weapons the Norman gripped
the hilt of his dagger, the only weapon he had with
him, and when his eyes caught the fierce looks bent
in his direction, he inwardly cursed his folly for
venturing among such savages so slenderly armed.
His fears, however, proved needless.   At a sign from
Gurth, every knife was sheathed, and he himself

stepped forwards to greet the smith and the Norman stranger. Meanwhile, Sir John had made some hasty explanation about the effect of a war-song upon men regaled with choice feastings. The Norman made a fitting reply, and the incident seemed ended.

A moment's time sufficed for an explanation of the smith's early return. He had seized upon the first opportunity the conversation offered for mentioning Gurth, and the king had at once expressed a desire to see the young thane.

" So," said Sir John, " I came at once to fetch thee, for we Saxons are in excellent odour just now, whilst the proud Normans stink somewhat in the kingly nostrils, for they have taken open offence at the marks of favour he hath bestowed upon many citizens since the court hath been here."

Gurth expressed himself as ready on the instant to accompany the smith, and so, taking no other retinue than the giant craftsman, Halford, the singer of " the song of the Wulf," he set out for the abbey.

His steps were directed to the chapter-room where the court was holden, and without delay he was ushered into the presence of the king. The stout smith acted as his herald and sponsor.

William, who had a quick eye for a manly form and honest face, smiled approvingly on Gurth's tall, sinewy frame, and fearless, handsome countenance. He called upon him to approach, and extended him his hand to kiss. Gurth made graceful homage, and, when he rose up again, William laid a hand on his shoulder, at the same time letting his eye rove over the faces of some of the surrounding Norman nobles.

"Thou art heartily welcome, noble thane," said he, deliberately and with emphasis. "We remember thy sire well, and the services thy house hath rendered us on this dangerous border. We are grieved to learn that thy sire is no more, but our grief is lessened now that we welcome thee and see that his lands and honours, and the keeping of our borders, are in such worthy hands. The brave Wulf of the Dean is welcome in our peaceful hall."

The king ceased speaking, and took his hand from Gurth's shoulder. The latter stepped back a pace or two, raised his blue eyes boldly to the king's face, and answered him in a voice as clear and ringing as his own.

"My lord king," cried he, "right gratefully do I thank thee for thy welcome and thy kindly words. Thou hast not forgotten our Forest home; we have not forgotten the king who graced it with his presence. If thou wilt deign again so to honour us, thou wilt find Forest hearts not less true and loyal than Norman ones."

"Of the truth of that we need no assurance," replied the king. "Moreover, we would have some talk with thee concerning the Forest and thy troublesome neighbours the Welsh. Stay thou here; we will have this talk anon."

The king then turned to one of his Norman knights, and held earnest conversation with him for some time. The courtiers, whenever possible, formed themselves into groups and discussed in angry whispers the king's flattering treatment of "these Saxon hogs."

Gurth, Sir John, Leofric, and some dignitaries of

the city who were present, chatted away in homely Saxon amidst the babel of French which was muttered around them. They kept their eyes open too, and were not slow to note and store up the malevolent glances cast in their direction.

Amongst the crowd of knights Gurth quickly distinguished his enemy, Gilbert of Tournay, and the young Norman whose wrist he had broken the previous evening. He smiled to think that at least one mincing foreigner bore the marks of Saxon prowess upon him.

Gilbert of Tournay kept his eye steadily upon the king. Suddenly, he broke from the group which surrounded him, and came towards the daïs. Gurth turned his head quickly in that direction. It was well that he did so. The king was alone, but, catching his eager glance, smiled, and beckoned him to approach. The advancing Norman stopped, bit his lip, turned sharply on his heel, and went back to his companions.

These suggestive movements were not lost upon Gurth, and he resolved his enemy should not forestall him. He went to the king's side.

"And now," said the latter, "thou shalt at the first tell thine own tale in thine own way. Questions may come afterwards. How stand affairs on our Forest border, and what things have happened there of late?"

Gurth gave the king as close an account as his memory permitted of the events of the last few years. Every raid and foray was mentioned, and the names and doings of all men who bore a prominent part therein.

Several times the king gave vent to a sharp "Ha ! " of surprise. He scanned Gurth's face closely, and seemed to keep back questions only with an effort.

"Thy tale is a strange one!" cried he, as soon as Gurth ceased speaking. "What part hath the knight Gilbert of Tournay played in these matters ? Thou dost not mention his name."

"He hath done nothing to the king's advantage," replied Gurth. "But I would crave thy patience on that point. I shall have much to say concerning him, if the king will but listen."

"We will find a time for all things," replied William. "Now, of another man. Thou hast spoken oft, and in terms of high praise, of Orcar the thane, whose lands lie at the Forest border. We have heard no good of this man. How dost thou know thy tale is the true one ? "

"Because the thane Orcar is my godfather and friend, the defender of my mother's widowhood and my father's name. Let but the king go down to the border and ask whom all men look to as their leader and defender; let him ask of the Welsh what name is a terror amongst them, what arm a scourge ! Every lip shall answer ' Orcar.' "

Gurth spoke earnestly and warmly, and his manner impressed the king.

"I believe thy tale," said he. "But there are some false knaves abroad. Now, what hast thou to say of Gilbert of Tournay ? "

"I would rather say my say openly and to his face," answered Gurth ; "for I have to charge him with abuses of power, plotting against the weal of the king's faithful subjects, and of other base and cowardly acts which brand him 'nithing.' It was for that end that I came unattended to the king's court, trusting in his justice and protection."

"Thou shalt have thy wish at once," replied William, rising hastily, his face set and stern. "Follow thou me. Tell the knight of Tournay we would have instant speech with him," continued he, turning to an attendant who stood near.

He left the room, Gurth following. In a few moments Gilbert of Tournay stood before them. The tale of the latter's misdeeds was then told ; his oppressions, robberies, torturings, his neglect of the border, his secret leagues with the king's enemies, whereby he incited them to make raids on the king's lands and plunder and slay his Saxon subjects.

William's face grew black as midnight, and his eyes roved angrily from accuser to accused.

Then Gurth came to the list of personal wrongs. The insults to his mother, the sneers, the gibes, the petty tyrannies, the threats were all poured into the ear of the king. The young thane's eyes flashed and his nostrils quivered with rage as the cowardly story was unfolded. The king watched his face with the keenest interest, and when he had finished, and before the Norman could reply, his anger blazed forth.

"By my kingly honour ! " he cried, " but this shall be answered for ! First, thou shalt answer to the Lady of the Dean for thy insults by the champion whom she shall appoint, and if God leave enough of thy false carcass for other vengeance to be wreaked upon, it shall not escape mine."

But so cool a villain as the knight of Tournay was not to be brushed aside lightly. He met the royal outburst calmly enough.

"Since when," said he, "hath the king of England taken to condemn, unheard, a belted knight to the forfeiture of honour and life? There is but sorry justice in a court where an untried, hot-headed strip-ling may swear away the life of a man of proved honour."

The king took no offence at the speech. He simply remarked, "There would be more point in thy plea, if I had not already proved thee unfaithful and forgetful of honour. Still thy defence shall be heard; but it would prove me a sorry king if even the untried stripling could not get justice at my hands. What hast thou to say?"

"That the Saxon youth hath a marvellous imagina-tion and gift of words, and a remarkable talent for lying. It were easy to spoil his pretty tale, if the Forest were at the door. Proofs must wait. I can at least show what manner of youth he is. He hath not been in the city three days; I will give three instances of his uprightness and loyalty whilst he has been near to the king's presence. The king may then judge what his doings are like to be when scores of leagues separate him from the royal eye and arm.

"Yesternight he waylaid my cousin, even in the abbey precincts, fell foully upon him from behind, felled him to the ground and broke his wrist. Ronald de Tarbeux is here, maimed, to attest the deed. This morning he attacked my page, a mere child, whose only offence was the wearing of my livery, and threw him into the frozen river. This very night, at the smith's house in Eadburga Street, taking advantage of the master's absence to wait upon his king, he incited the men-servants to sing rebellious songs, and to draw their daggers upon the king's messenger, Sir Rollo, knight of Caen, who stood for some moments, unarmed, and in peril of his life."

"How now?" cried the king sharply, his face working with anger and perplexity; "these are pointed charges! What hast thou to say to them?"

Gurth's answer was sharp and hot. "They are false! every one of them," he cried; "and Gilbert of Tournay is unworthy of his knighthood, for he is liar! coward! nithing! And with your leave, my lord king, I will prove him so ere I leave your presence this night."

"That thou shalt do, whether thou likest it or no!" cried William grimly. "I have had enow and to spare of these cross-accusations."

"Then I ask that this knight's cousin and page be summoned, also the knight of Caen, Sir John the Smith, his daughter Elgiva, and Halford, the Smith's man who attended me hither to-night."

"The matter shall be tried in full court," replied the king.

He arose, and went back to the chapter-room, and at once gave orders for the witnesses to be brought.

Halford the smith was near at hand, and was the first placed under examination. Gurth, who brought him forward as the minstrel of the supper, declined to ask him any questions, leaving that entirely to the king and his accuser. The latter at once demanded

5

that the words of the song should be repeated in open court.

Halford, wondering what was the matter with his minstrelsy, complied. The king listened intently, but found no treason in the words. Then Gurth explained that it was simply the war-song of his house, and that, as such, it had been sung for centuries.

Gilbert, however, still persisted that the song was sung on this occasion with treasonable intent, and demanded an explanation of the meditated attack on the king's messenger.

Gurth again referred the king to Halford. When the latter was made to understand the purport of the charges, he waxed indignant.

"We had nought but good in our hearts towards the king," he cried, " seeing the great honour he had done to our craft and our master. There is no smith in the west, now, that would not give his life for him. We drew our knives when we drank wassail to our young lord. We saw no Norman, and our thoughts were not towards the Norman when we sang, but only towards the beggarly Welsh."

The evident honesty of the outburst satisfied the king. He frowned darkly upon Gilbert, and bade him say no more upon the charge.

By this time the page had been dragged sleepily and full of terror from his bed. Hurried before the court, and seeing none but angry, glowering faces around him, his terror increased. At the first harsh words from the king's lips he began to whimper.

"Make the brat hold his peace and attend to me," cried William, stamping his foot.

There was instant silence.

"Look here, sirrah!" he continued, "and keep thine eyes from thy master's face. Who threw thee into the river yesterday? and why wert thou thrown? Answer me truthfully, or I'll have the flesh whipped from thy bones!"

The poor page sank to his knees. Gasping with terror, he told the true story, and not the one his master had diligently rehearsed with him. At its close there was a silence as of death in the room. Contrary to expectation, William did not speak, but the expression on his face sent a shudder through every heart. He motioned them to carry the terror-stricken page from his presence. He looked enquiringly at Gurth. The latter answered the look.

"I await the coming of the smith's daughter," he said.

There was silence again for many minutes. At last hurrying steps were heard in the cloister without. The curtains were drawn aside, and Elgiva, warmly hooded and cloaked, entered on the arm of her father. Room was made for her immediately before the king. Trembling with vague apprehensions she stood there, for she did not know why she was summoned. Seeing Gurth standing near her, she instinctively guessed that the matter concerned him.

"Throw back thy hood, fair maid," said William with unusual gentleness, "thou hast nothing to fear."

Elgiva obeyed.

The vision of so fair and sweet a face, emerging to the light of the flaring, smoking torches, caused a faint murmur of pleased surprise to go round the

room.   The smith drew himself a little more proudly
up, and the king's face sensibly softened.

"What dost thou wish with her?" he said to
Gurth.

"That she may be confronted by the Norman with
the broken wrist," he replied.

Ronald de Tarbeux was called forward.   He came
with a somewhat ill grace.   The penetrating look the
king gave him did not increase his sense of comfort.

As he came towards Elgiva, she shrank back nearer
to Gurth; and the king did not fail to notice the
instinctive action.   The latter looked for Gurth to
begin.

"My lord," said he, "again I do not wish to put
my word against the word of my accuser.   I have
given him the lie already.   Will it please you to ask
this maiden what she knows of the man before her?"

"Thou hearest the question, maiden," said William;
"what answer canst thou give to it?"

Gurth's reply to the king let Elgiva into the whole
secret of her presence before him.   She threw her
fears to the winds, and determined to speak out.   She
raised her eyes to the king's, her face suffused with
burning blushes, and told him the whole story.

The king stepped down from his seat, and took her
hands in his.

"Little one," he said, "it grieves me that so much
sweetness and innocence suffered from the rudeness
of follower of mine.   I owe thee reparation.   Thou
shalt have it.   Nay, frown not, Sir John, a younger,
and mayhap more favoured arm than thine hath well
avenged the insult.   And now, fair maid, I give thee

'good-night'; I have words to say that I would not thine ears should hear."

With a low curtsey, Elgiva took her departure. Immediately the mood of the king changed. The velvet glove had been displayed; now they felt the hand of iron. For an hour his court trembled before him. The storm had been brewing for days; now it burst over them with terrific fury.

They found that the Duke of Normandy was not only the Conqueror, but the King of England, and moreover that he intended to reign as king over Saxons as well as Normans, and Normans as well as Saxons. However much they disliked the position, he placed them side by side with the despised Saxons as a people obeying the same laws and subject to the same restrictions. A loyal Saxon was as dear in his eyes as a loyal Norman, and their property, honour, lives, just as precious in his sight.

At the end of his stormy harangue, he poured forth such a torrent of threats and imprecations against those offenders who stood before him, that their hearts melted within them. Then he turned to Gurth, and praised him without stint. He applauded his bravery, his modesty and his devotion; he referred with a glow of pride to the young thane's fearless trust in a king's power and justice, a trust which had brought him unattended, almost unarmed to the court, and with nought but the virtue of a good cause to support him.

"Such," he cried, "are the hearts I want about me. Such are the men to whom honour and reward shall come."

He turned to the knight of Tournay.

"I had purposed," he said, "to make thee warden of the Forest Marches ; but I find thee so false and perjured, that thou mayest count things well with thee if I do no more than hang thee in the market-place like a thieving cur. Upon him whom thou wouldst have basely betrayed shall the honour fall ; an honour he might claim as his right, for his family hath alway faithfully maintained such a trust since the days of Alfred."

William then ordered the two offending Normans to be placed under closest arrest, and, having thrown out a few more pointed and significant hints to his silent nobles, he left the room.

Followed by looks of deadly hate, and many muttered threats, Gurth and the whole of the Saxons went out immediately after him.

But the sense of a great triumph went with them, and so they minded scowls and curses but little.

Accompanied by the watchful giant, Halford, Gurth strode off through the winter night to recount the full measure of his victory to the anxious smith. Meanwhile Elgiva's story had run like a fire through the house, and he arrived at Eadburga Street to find himself a hero indeed.

CHAPTER VI.

THE next morning, Gurth arose with a light heart. He was the first of all the household to be astir.

Now that his errand was successfully accomplished, he wished to be home again. City life was not to the liking of the free young forester. More than all he was eager to gladden his mother's heart with the news of the king's graciousness.

The Forest, too, would rejoice to know that its ancient liberties were still under the protection of its natural and rightful lord. But for this royal confirmation of the dignities of his house, the young thane would have commenced his homeward journey at sunrise. Now, he knew he must await the pleasure of the king.

As soon as the smith appeared, he took counsel with him concerning his future movements. Sir John advised him to seek an early audience with the king, and endeavour to get all things settled beyond question or dispute.

" 'Strike whilst the iron is hot,' is ever the smith's motto," said he.

The advice agreed exactly with Gurth's temper at the moment. For one thing the position of Gilbert de Tournay did not give him unmingled satisfaction. He did not want his personal quarrel with that knight swallowed up in the giant maw of kingly anger. So he determined to go to the abbey at noon and crave audience of the Conqueror.

By the time this decision was arrived at, the whole household was up and ready for the morning meal.

The revelry and excitement of the previous night sat heavily on most of the company. Little was eaten, but the energies saved over mastication were more than spent upon speech. It was a company exceedingly prodigal of words.

At noon, Gurth wended his way to the abbey. He was admitted to the king's presence almost immediately. William greeted him warmly, and readily entered into conversation concerning the wardenship, its limits, and the large powers rightly attaching to it. Much sound advice he gave respecting the tactics to be followed in dealing with the ever-watching and ever-warring Welsh ; but, most valuable of all, he counselled the youthful warden respecting his associates in power, especially those of Norman blood, who would be but ill-disposed to place themselves at any time under the banner of a Saxon chieftain. He displayed great interest in the past glories and present fame of the house of Wulf, and warmly enjoined upon the young thane that he should strive to add to its record of fair and honourable renown, and let no ignoble deed cast one blot upon it.

Gurth thanked him humbly, yet heartily, for his

exceeding graciousness, and then ventured upon the other matter which so nearly concerned him.

" I would crave some words with you, my lord," said he, "touching this Gilbert of Tournay, who hath played me and mine so foul a game."

William's brow darkened instantly.

" Thou needst not fear for him," answered he ; "he hath played us too foul a game to have the chance given him to play us another."

" It is for that reason that I desire to speak of him," replied Gurth, "and I beg that my king will not judge me presumptuous in speaking as I crave to do."

" Say on."

" This man hath wounded our house in its dearest and most precious part ; he hath vilely insulted her who is more to me than all else on earth. Such deeds should be requited at mine own hands."

" For that cause we should have justice upon him. He hath done wrong to loyal subjects of ours whom it is our bounden duty to protect. He hath also been guilty of something very like treason."

" Then I crave my petition as a boon from the king."

" He will refuse thee combat. Thou art not of knightly rank."

" The king hath given me chance to win my spurs."

" But thou art still many years from knightly age."

" Time will pass quickly when a great work awaits the doing. Let but the king say that the day shall come, and I am content."

William pondered a moment before replying. " I

will grant thy boon in so far that we will not claim our due of him until thou hast had chance to demand thine."

Gurth thanked the king, and then prepared to depart. He was commanded, however, not to leave the city until he had received under the king's own seal the full title of his wardenship, and a description of the powers belonging thereto.

Finding it impossible to get away from the city at once, Gurth sent a messenger to the Dean to acquaint its lady with the good fortune which had attended his mission. Then, to while away the time of his enforced stay the more pleasantly, he set up a target in the meadow at the rear of the smith's house, and daily instructed Edwy in throwing the javelin and shooting at a mark. Oftentimes some of the smith's men and apprentices joined them, and shooting, throwing, and hurling matches were indulged in, to the great delight and profit of all.

The huge Halford, who, since the night of the feast had become intensely attached to Gurth, made himself the devoted slave of the two lads.

Finding that the ordinary javelin was much too heavy for Edwy's strength, he procured some small wands of light, tough wood, and fashioning steel heads to correspond, made him a half-score of admirable weapons, for what they lacked in weight and force they made up in the exquisite temper and point of the steel. Gurth's sword, too, was, under the master hand of Leofric, rapidly approaching completion. And all the while, taking advantage of the extension of his stay, the generous smith and two of his best workmen were busily preparing another happy surprise for the young thane.

The time of departure came at length. In the forenoon of the 24th day of December, two ponies and a stout horse stood ready saddled in the court-yard of the smithy, a group of workmen and apprentices gathered round them.

Halford, clad in a leathern jerkin and stout woollen trews, a light steel cap upon his head, a huge axe in his hand, stood ready prepared for a journey. Being a freeman, and bound in no way to the smith's service, he had decided to quit it and link his fortunes once again to the house of Wulf. The boys hailed his decision with delight.

Soon the rest of the little cavalcade appeared, accompanied by their host and hostess and Elgiva. A shout of greeting went up at the sight of Gurth, and another shout for Sir John when it was seen how their young Forest lord was dressed. His body was clad in a corselet of beautifully-fashioned chain mail, lined with fine wool of a sufficient thickness in itself to turn the point of an arrow or javelin ; a steel cap similarly quilted covered his head. These were the surprise gifts of his warm-hearted host ; and a magnificently-hilted sword hung at his side. A proud lad was the young thane of Wulf that day, for, in a leathern wallet at his girdle lay the charter of his wardenship of the Dean Forest and the Forest Marches.

Edwy walked with Elgiva, proudly bearing his bundle of javelins. Both lads warmly embraced Sir John and his wife and daughter, and with a hearty farewell to all, vaulted into their saddles and rode briskly off, Halford riding a few paces in the rear. Tears dimmed one pair of bright eyes as their forms disappeared at the turning into the Westgate Street.

The smith looked at the sky.

"It is well that they stayed no longer," said he, "for methinks to-morrow will see the Forest paths lost in a shroud of snow."

Dame Alicia echoed his words, but her thoughts added another reason why they should be gone.

"My little maid was losing her heart," she said to herself.

Elgiva sighed.

"My heart hath ridden away with my lord," she whispered. "The All-Father grant that no harm happen to him, or I am undone for ever."

The little cavalcade rode sharply down the sloping roadway, on past the abbey, down to the Westgate. They passed quickly through, and over the Westgate Bridge, just giving a glance at the turbid river flowing seawards below. They clattered along the causeway of the marshy island of Olney, crossed the western arm of the river, and came out upon the high road leading to Newnham, Littledean, the Forest itself, and the distant Welsh border. The city was now completely hidden from view.

"Hurrah for the oak and the holly green!" sang Edwy. "Come, Gurth, what sayest thou to a rousing gallop?"

"I am with thee," replied Gurth.

A shaking of the reins, a sharp word of command,

and each little pony started forward like a stone from a sling. For the next two miles the boys raced onward at a fair gallop, laughing heartily at Halford's attempts to force his heavy steed along at a somewhat equal rate.

With merry laugh and gay chatter they sped along, and soon the dark belt of Forest rose on the horizon before them. By this time the wind had risen somewhat, and was wailing mournfully through the coppices by the roadside. Ever and anon, fine snowflakes fell coldly and softly on their faces.

At length they struck across the open country towards the Severn bank, and following the winding river-path, came upon the cluster of fisher-huts belonging to the thane Orcar. In a few minutes more, they had ridden up to the gate in the stout palisade surrounding the house.

The steward came forward to welcome them, but he brought the intelligence that his master was not at home. News had been brought to the effect that two bands of Welsh, under the brothers ap Morgan, had crossed the Wye, so Orcar had ridden off to the Dean.

The riders dismounted and entered the house, but although urgently pressed to break their journey until the morrow, they decided to press on as soon as they and their steeds were refreshed. A storm was fast coming up, and in a few hours the Forest tracks might be obliterated by the snow. There was a bright moon, so they had no fear of the on-coming of night.

The sun had just dropped down behind the vast

expanse of bare tree-tops as they defiled off along the narrow bridle path to Littledean.

At a distance of a quarter of an hour's ride along this path another woodland track ˮof about equal width opened into it. This led almost in a bee line to the Gloncester Road, which road it entered about two miles before Newnham. It afforded a short cut to those who wished to avoid the winding river-path, and also a means of approach to the Forest for those who had no very ardent wish for a meeting with the thane Orcar or his men.

It was for this latter reason that four Norman horsemen rode rapidly along it whilst Gurth and his companions were enjoying their brief rest and refreshment at Newnham. The riders reached the angle of the two paths and halted.

"Shall we wait here, Gilbert?" said one. He was none other than our old acquaintance Ronald de Tarbeux, his hand bandaged, and tied in a silken scarf across his breast.

"No!" answered de Tournay. "It is too open for one thing, and too near the 'sty of the Newnham boar' for another. Orcar is likely enough to accompany his precious charges thus far. We must make no slip this time, or our good and sweet-tempered king will dangle us from one of these stout oaks. I have no relish for playing the part of acorn. We will ride another mile or so farther along the Forest path."

Acting upon this determination, the two knights and their attendant men-at-arms turned into the path and rode on.

We will explain the unexpected appearance of these

knights in the Forest. Unfortunately for Gurth, the king had listened only too well to his request for a stay of execution upon de Tournay. William was averse to judicial bloodshed, and this particular follower had often rendered him excellent service. He had therefore soundly rated him, and satisfied his anger by setting him at liberty with a threat of the worst consequences should any further complaint of ill-doing be made against him. The morning of his liberation was the morning of Gurth's departure from the city. A watch had been kept on the young Saxon, and within an hour after his passing through the city gate, his worst enemies had ridden through in pursuit, intent upon his destruction. They were fully alive to the truth of the proverb, " Dead men tell no tales."

As soon as Gurth and his companion had got well into the shadow of the Forest, the evening sky became suddenly overcast, quite vanquishing their hopes of effective moonlight, and the snow, which had long threatened, began to fall heavily. This was unfortunate, even for those accustomed to woodland life and woodland ways.

" We must ride hard," said Gurth, and he pressed his willing little steed forward.

On, along the grassy track, they cantered, the footfalls of the horses becoming fainter and fainter as the snowy carpet thickened. They reached the junction of the paths. The trees creaked and groaned in the increasing gale, and the thick flakes swirled blindingly around them. They had a moment's difficulty in finding the right opening amongst the trees.

"We are safe as far as Littledean," said Halford; "there are no turnings to lead us astray."

"On, then!" cried Gurth, "at the best speed we can make."

They went now at a hand-gallop, Gurth leading, and Halford bringing up the rear. But the storm swept so thickly down the narrow alley that they were enshrouded in an almost impenetrable veil of snow. Another furlong would bring them to where their foes lay ambushed; but, heedless of all enemies save the snow and the darkness, they sped swiftly along, silent and ghostly.

The Normans lay hidden in the thickets, two on either side of the narrow path. Giving no warning of their approach, the Saxons were upon them and beyond them before they were aware. They saw a thick mass of snow pass by, and that was all. But this all was sufficient for a watchful enemy. Halford had hardly got a dozen yards beyond the place of ambush, when he heard an order to "mount and ride" given sharply in French. He turned in his saddle, and his quick, forest-trained eye saw the whole thing in an instant. He uttered no sound, but forced his horse forward until he was abreast of Gurth.

"A trap, my lord!" he cried, pointing behind him. "They missed us, but are giving chase."

"Norman or Welsh?"

"Norman, my lord. Four men, mailed and mounted."

Gurth slackened the pace of his pony a little, and looked behind. Through the driving clouds of snow he could see nothing.

" We are safe enough, if we keep them at a fair distance behind us. They cannot see us, and this snow and winding path are better protection than ditch and rampart. Get thou in front, Edwy, and gallop hard."

Away they sped again. Over the horses they bent, their faces raised only so much as would enable them to peer into the fleecy clouds before them. They felt, rather than saw their way, and trusted greatly to the instinct of their steeds. Halford, riding along in the rear, smiled grimly as the thought struck him that no missile would be likely to pass his burly form in this narrow path. He felt that the two lads were perfectly safe.

The Normans were by this time mounted, and their horses, whose hoofs were so far free from snow, began to gain ground at once. The pursuers rode hard, trusting to fortune to preserve them from broken necks.

Halford strained his ears to catch every sound. For some minutes he heard nothing but the noise of the storm and the footfalls of his own horse. Something came ripping through the branches, and stuck, with a dull thud, into a stout limb close to the left of him. He turned his head sharply.

" So ho !" muttered he, " a spear ! "

He pushed on more quickly. He reached Gurth.

" Thy javelin," he said.

Gurth thrust it out behind him. Halford fell back a little. As far as he could judge, a long straight piece of path lay before them.

Another spear came hurtling through the trees, this time some yards to the right of him. The path

6

had just swept round a bend to the left. The weapon, however, came with much greater force. Either a stronger arm had hurled it, or the pursuers had gained very considerably.

He rode on. Presently he reined up. He judged that fifty good yards of straight path lay behind him. He raised himself in his stirrups, and the javelin flew with terrific force from his hand. Without waiting to judge its effect, he went forward again with a bound. He heard nothing. He had misjudged then ; the pursuers were not in the straight. He must try again. By an effort he reached the lads.

"Some more spears!" he cried.

Gurth reached forward, took some from Edwy's sheath, and handed them behind as he had previously done.

"Push on!" exclaimed the stout henchman.

He halted at the spot. He waited and listened, leaning intently over his horse's crupper. A moment more, and he was erect in the stirrups again, and, in quick succession, three of the spears he had fashioned, were launched into the veil behind.

He paused an instant.

"*Diable!*" shouted an angry voice.

"Hit!" cried Halford.

Another spear flew from his hand.

Another oath was rapped sharply out.

Two spears whizzed past him, one within an inch of his head. He turned and rode forward at a gallop, lying flat down upon his horse's back. The figures of the flying lads loomed mistily before him. He raised himself again.

" On! on !" he shouted.

Then he swerved from the path to the side of a huge spreading beech. Another project had entered his mind. He was tired of unseen foes. The tree trunk was betwixt him and his pursuers. He took his great axe from his belt, and swung it round in his hand.

A galloping was audible. Then voices. They drew nearer. He gripped reins and axe more tightly, and settled himself more firmly in the saddle. A white galloping figure loomed out. He was leading. Halford grinned.

An instant more, and a terrific cry, " A Wulf !" rang out. Horse and rider leapt across the path. The mighty axe fell with a " swish," and went crashing through the skull of the Norman's steed. Down he went like a log, carrying his rider with him, and effectually barring the path. Just as swiftly Halford dashed forward again, and was lost in the storm.

Cries and curses followed him. He rode on now at a headlong pace. He caught up his young masters.

" One is down, my lord," he panted, " and the path is blocked. Our numbers are equal, and if it were not for the young Edwy, I should say, let us wait and fight them."

" That is it," said Gurth bitterly. " Were it not for my brother's youth, I would not have ridden a foot from the cowards. It irks me sorely, a Wulf, to run from Norman robbers. By my father's soul, though, I will turn and meet them, if they pursue us farther."

" Good !" ejaculated Halford. " Let us ride slower,

my horse is giving out ; my bulk is not a light load to fly with."

They reined their steeds in a little, and rode more leisurely.

"We are not far from Littledean," said Gurth. "Mayhap, they will give up the chase."

This idea proved ill-founded. In a little while shouts came borne along on the wind, which told that the pursuit was being followed more keenly and fiercely than ever.

"Edwy," cried Gurth, "keep well to the front, and prepare thyself to obey instantly whatever commands I shall give thee."

"Have no fear !" answered the youngster heartily ; "I am prepared. Thou shalt find that I can hit a fair mark truly."

They rode on more quickly, but with no ultimate intention of flying. The pursuit came on, nearer and nearer. Gurth eagerly peered into the bushes and trees that lined the path.

Suddenly he called, "Halt !"

He decided to await the enemy here. His plan was thought out ; and in a few quiet sentences it was arranged.

"Place thyself at the farther side of this clump of firs to the left," he said to Edwy. "They are good cover. Get ready thy best-pointed spear. Hurl it at the face of the man who shall be brought up opposite to thee. If thou canst not do this, then make a target of his horse. Thou wilt but waste thy small strength against his body. Thou, Halford, take thy stand a few paces farther on, on the right

side of the way. Thy work will be to block the path,
bring these fellows to a stand, and engage the leading
one. I will post myself on the side of the fir clump
and dash across the crupper of the hindmost horse.
Each must look to his own man. They cannot see
us in this blinding storm. We have them as they
thought to have us, and must not fail to bring them
down. Now to cover ! "

" They are as dead as King Alfred," chuckled
Halford, as he rode to his post.

For some minutes there was silence, save for the
shrieks and howls and groans of the storm-swept
Forest. The three Saxons sat their horses, brushed
the snow from their faces, and with nerves strained
to the highest tension, waited and listened for the
oncoming of their foes.

" Hist ! the muffled gallop of horses."

Each gripped his weapon, and Halford and Gurth
braced their steeds for the spring.

They heard the quick panting of hard-pressed
animals.

A white mass swept to the fir clump. It passed
Gurth. A fearful yell, " A Wulf ! A Wulf ! "
and Halford was across the path. The head of the
Norman's horse was within a foot of him. It swerved,
reared, plunged. He was prepared for all. He rose
in his stirrups. The fearful axe whirled round his
head, and before the Norman could raise a hand to
defend himself, it came down like a gleaming thunder-
bolt. Without having uttered a sound, the foeman
dropped lifeless to the ground. The horse dashed
into the bushes.

Halford tightened his grip on his weapon, and turned to see how his companions were faring. He turned at the nick of time.

Edwy had cast his spear at the second horseman, who was none other than de Tournay himself. But the lad's nerves were too strained for a steady aim, and the missile flew harmlessly across the Norman's face.

Quick as thought de Tournay turned to the direction whence it came. Edwy was in the act of snatching another spear from his bundle.

There was not a moment to lose. The Norman clapped his sword across his horse's neck, seized a mace which hung at his saddle, and whirled it ready for a throw. In another moment the hapless youngster would have been dashed to the ground a bruised and lifeless mass.

But it was at that moment that Halford saw his danger and the Norman's intention. His axe was ready, and with lightning instinct it was hurled from his hand. It struck the Norman across the ribs and under the armpit of his raised arm. The ribs cracked beneath the corselet, and the force of the blow sent him spinning from his stirrups, headlong into the snow.

Meanwhile, Gurth was engaged in a hot hand-to-hand encounter with the third horseman, a strapping man-at-arms. Riding last, the fellow had received more warning than his companions. He turned to face his assailant in an instant. It was hack, cut, thrust, on either side, and with but small advantage. The young thane was the nimbler, and his steed the more easily managed, but his antagonist was powerfully built, and a thorough swordsman. The double victory of Halford, however, decided the issue of this combat also. The fellow, seeing his case become desperate, made a rash lunge at Gurth's throat. The young thane not only parried it, but by a quick twist managed also to send his opponent's weapon flying from his grasp. The Norman, finding himself defenceless save for a small dagger he had snatched from his belt, threw this down also, and called for "quarter."

This was granted, and the prisoner having been dismounted and securely bound, Gurth turned with Halford to look at the condition of the two other assailants.

The first victim of the terrible axe, by his dress, and by the fact that one of his hands was bound up, proved to be that erstwhile gay spark of Norman knighthood, Sir Ronald de Tarbeux. They quickly put the ghastly object out of sight in the fir clump.

De Tournay they found alive, and with no worse injuries than a half-dazed brain and a couple of broken ribs. He was soon brought to his senses and placed on his horse. The other prisoner was mounted and tied to his saddle, and the little cavalcade set off again along the Forest path. Halford led the way, the two prisoners came next, and Gurth and Edwy brought up the rear.

"What wilt thou do with these men, Gurth?" asked Edwy as they rode along.

"Hang them!" replied he.

"Both?"

"Both. The king shall have early evidence that my wardenship of the Forest will be no idle one."

The Norman knight heard these words, and turned painfully in his saddle.

"Have a care, my young Sir Cockerel," he sneered, "that thou art not hanged first. Thou art like to be, unless thou speedily play accuser, judge, and executioner in thine own person."

"Thou wilt have a fair trial, Sir Norman, and an equally fair hanging!"

"Oh! What dost thou imagine a judge would say to thy story? Four men, proved warriors, waylay a boor, a boy, and a baby in the heart of a forest. Of the four stalwarts, but one escapes with a whole skin, whilst the three precious ones escape unscathed! Thou wilt want a mad judge and a jury of jesters to tell such twaddle to!"

Gurth bit his lips to keep back his wrath. "I'll bandy no words with thee," he answered.

Now fortune had not destined that Gurth should at this time enter the Dean in triumph. Her favours for the present were to partake more of the nature of kicks than halfpence.

The steed of de Tarbeux, dashing wildly on through the Forest, attracted by the neighing of its own kind, had galloped riderless into the camp of the younger ap Morgan, who lay hidden close to the Saxon village of Littledean, meditating an early raid upon the place.

The condition of the animal told its own tale, and just at that very moment when home and welcoming friends seemed almost in sight, our young thane rode unsuspectingly into a trap from which there was no escape.

A hundred skin-clad, grinning Welshmen suddenly surrounded both victors and vanquished. The three Saxons were dragged from their steeds and deprived of their weapons almost before they had realised the presence of their new and unexpected foes. For the Welshmen there was a strong element of humour in the situation.

Ap Morgan, by way of a rough jest, tied the Saxon thane and his knightly Norman prisoner together, and in this maddening position, propped up against the gnarled trunk of an oak, the snow falling heavily around him, Gurth spent the bitterest night of his life.

CHAPTER VII.

EARLY the next morning, the Welsh chieftain struck his camp and disappeared in the almost trackless Forest. He denied himself the pleasure of a raid upon the stockyards of Littledean in order to reach the Wye whilst the snow still fell heavily enough to obliterate the trail of his band. By noon, however, of the Christmas Day, the storm ceased entirely, and ap Morgan pushed on westwards more rapidly than ever. His band were mounted on sturdy Forest ponies, and, riding in single file, they left but little direct indication of their numbers.

The sun had gone down behind the steep, wooded hills on the western bank when they filed out on the eastern side of the river. The waters were low and easily fordable. The Welshmen crossed quickly. Then leisurely they wound up the steep path, disappeared over the summit, and struck off to the small fort of the Morgans, a few miles to the south-west of Ross. Gurth could not forbear a sigh when he rode down the slope ; he felt that friends and Christmas cheer were far away indeed, when forest, river, and hill lay between him and them.

He, Edwy, and Halford rode together unbound,

94

but unarmed and well-guarded. They were quit of the unwelcome society of de Tournay, who rode at the head of the troop with the leader, endeavouring to carry on an intelligible conversation with him. The Norman man-at-arms, following the example of his leader, was likewise zealously endeavouring to make himself agreeable to his captors. The Saxons rode moodily along, and for the most part silent.

When the Welshman's stronghold was reached, he showed no present purpose of ill-treating his prisoners. The Saxons were well lodged. The Normans were allowed to wander about at will, and de Tournay found a seat at the chief's table. The young thane noticed this, and felt that it boded no good to him. Could he have heard the conversation that went on between these two amidst the uproar of the Christmas feast, he would have seen cause for the gravest anxiety. With all the venom of a defeated coward, and all the plausibility of an accomplished rascal, the Norman was striving to urge ap Morgan to hang his three hereditary foes off-hand.

The mind of the Welshman was, however, much too politic for any such rashness. The Norman's promise of alliance and protection he secretly laughed at, and he had no great idea of his pluck or honesty ; moreover, he knew too well the vicissitudes of border warfare to make his own capture at any future time the certain prelude to a long rope dance from a limb of a forest oak. So he bluntly refused to be made the Norman's cat's-paw. One important arrangement, however, he agreed to. The Normans were to be given their liberty on the morrow, and an escort to guide them safely through the Forest to de Tournay's castle.

The Norman on his part agreed to keep ap Morgan acquainted with what went on at the Dean, to help him with a picked body of men in his next raid in the marches, and to claim no share of the plunder.

The next morning de Tournay crossed the Wye again, his mind full of schemes for the undoing of the house of Wulf.

A week passed away. Ap Morgan declared he was " the happiest man alive." Gurth thought he was the most miserable. At the Dean the anxiety was acute. As soon as the storm abated, scouts were sent out along the Forest paths. They found ample signs of the Welsh camp at Littledean ; and to a forester's eye their homeward trail was as plain as the sun at noon. However, they made no attempt to follow the marauders. Along the main path to Newnham they found nothing to aid their search until they came to the scene of the fight. There, evidences of a struggle were unmistakable. A suspicious looking heap in the fir-clump was found to be the dead body of the Norman. The thane Orcar, who led the search party, at once declared the awful death blow to be no Welsh-man's work. The dead body of the horse next rewarded their efforts. Again the Norman had suffered. Then a javelin was found firmly fixed in the trunk of a tree. Norman again. Next, two of Edwy's small spears were discovered similarly embedded. Lastly, one was picked up and identified on all hands as belonging to Gurth.

The party turned and rode home again, one man

only being dispatched to Newnham to see what tidings could be gleaned in that quarter. As they approached Littledean, a sharp pair of eyes amongst them detected signs of the Welsh ambuscade. Then the main parts of the grim Christmas-eve story stood revealed. The Lady of the Dean met them at the outer gate of the palisade.

"What news?" she asked anxiously.

"Good news and ill news!" replied Orcar. "The lads entered the Forest yester-e'en accompanied by some stout fellow, either of my house-carles, or from the smith's. They were pursued by Normans, at least two of them. There was a running fight along the path. The lads won, for we found one Norman horse with a well-cracked skull, and further on a Norman knight lying unburied with his cowardly pate equally well cloven. I would give something to see the arm that struck the blows. The lads fought well, too, as these spears show."

"But where are my brave boys, good thane?" interrupted the Lady Marian, clasping her hands.

Orcar's brow fell. "That I can only guess at," said he. "We found the ap Morgans had been abroad at Littledean."

"And they have taken them?"

"E'en so!"

The tears welled to the mother's eyes. "My poor Edwy!" she murmured.

"Fret not, dame," said Orcar gently; "they shall share Christmas cheer with us, if we partake not of it till Twelfth-tide. We will track the Welsh fox at once."

A small party was soon sent out to follow up the Welshman's trail. The sun had gone down and the moon had risen ere they returned. Their foes had made good their escape.

Meanwhile the messenger came back from Newnham. He brought important news. The Norman, whose horse had fallen beneath the brawny arm of Halford, had been found by one of Orcar's swineherds early in the morning almost frozen to death. He was coming to the Dean under escort as soon as he had sufficiently recovered the use of his limbs.

That night the dwellers at the Dean and the miners of Cinderford were all astir. They had received a summons to arms for day-dawn on the morrow. The news spread like wildfire, and the whole Forest was soon in a ferment. Men vowed vengeance and, instead of "Wassail" to their friends, drank "Death!" to the Welsh and Normans in their horns of Christmas mead and ale.

Women urged their brothers, sons, and husbands to the fight, for, was not their beloved and widowed lady bereft of her sons? and was not their brave young lord a captive? And the morning dawned in another blinding snowstorm which raged for days. Then for days the Forest paths were impassable, and the stout foresters ate out their hearts in their impatience.

The New Year came, and still the would-be rescuers were as fast bound as the prisoners they would release. At last came the welcome thaw.

A hundred strong, the foresters and miners assembled in the courtyard of the Forest fortress.

With a ringing cheer for their lady and her daughter,

who stood and waved them adieu, they turned, and, headed by the burly Orcar, wound out in long files over the drawbridge, and disappeared into the dark mass of the trees, wending their way along the wet and miry paths towards the river.

Behind them, under a strong guard, remained the Norman man-at-arms. His story of the treachery and treason of de Tournay had excited such resentment, that that knight's life was not worth a moment's purchase if any retainer of the house of Wulf got a clear aim at him with spear or arrow.

The Norman, snowed up with his Welsh escort, was busily employed, and the Saxons were soon to hear of him and to some purpose. Orcar knew not that such a crafty foe lay to the rear of him.

CHAPTER VIII.

IT was on the tenth day after Christmas that Orcar and his band set out bent upon the liberation of the Saxon captives.

Reaching the river late in the forenoon, he found it swollen and muddy, the stream running very strongly, and breast high even at the ford. Therefore he set about making a pathway at once. The banks were high and rocky, and huge blocks of red sandstone easily obtainable. Spreading his men about in parties amongst the trees and thick undergrowth, they laboured on, and by an hour before sunset had collected such a store of rock that a causeway might be constructed in a very short space of time.

Then a half-score of men were sent across to bring report of the enemy. They spread themselves out as far as the hill-top, but found the whole sodden, wintry landscape devoid of any sign of man. Then the Saxons hurled down the largest rocks into the river; and each man working in his appointed place silently and swiftly, before the last streak of red had faded from the sky a causeway stretched across the stream, wherein they might walk two abreast, and no man be knee-deep in the swift, icy waters.

Leaving a small but picked band to guard each end of the ford, the thane marshalled at the top of the western slope, and, keeping well hidden on the crest, waited for the moon to get above the horizon, for he proposed paying a night visit to the fox in his den. While he waits for the silver lamp to rise above the dark tree-tops we will see how Gurth is faring after his ten days' captivity.

From the first he and Halford had plotted escape. Guard was by no means strictly kept, and the walls of their dungeon but wooden ones. It was situated in an angle of the low, rambling building. Halford declared that he could work his way through it with his brave axe in half an hour and make but little noise. Unfortunately the axe was now a treasured possession of ap Morgan himself.

Round the whole fortress ran a high, broad wall of large stones and earth ; beyond this a deep, wide ditch. But the wall was not beyond their scaling powers ; and all three were excellent swimmers. Their most powerful gaoler was the heavy mantle of snow outside, and this guard was strengthened by every thick-falling shower.

Ap Morgan knew this, and he and his gave themselves up to snug enjoyment. Once or twice Halford found opportunity to try his blandishments upon a plump, dark-eyed maiden who glanced up at the prisoners' lattice as she passed. But his efforts brought him nothing save a smile or two, a few shakes of a pretty head, and a musically-murmured " Dym Sassenach " (" I do not know English ").

But the thaw came ; the betraying, tell-tale snow

7

was disappearing. Guard was as loosely kept as ever. Gurth's hopes rose high.

A small but keen and excellently-tempered dagger in his belt had escaped the eyes of his captors. One edge of this Halford converted into a saw. He then traced out a square of about three feet in the outermost corner of their small cell. With the patience and care of a skilled, painstaking mechanic, he cut and sawed quite through the log walls on three sides of the square ; along the base he cut nearly through, but left the whole square in such a state that an aperture large enough for a quick escape could be made by a sharp kick or a steady pressure of knee or shoulder.

Then Gurth determined they should make a dash for freedom at the first opportunity. They had no hope of arming themselves for defence ; the game must be won by luck, speed, and stealth, or not at all. The chance came at last in the interval between sunset and moonrise, and at the very time when a hundred pairs of brave and friendly eyes were watching for the celestial signal to march to their rescue.

Halford unwound the deerskin straps from his legs. He fastened them together and formed a strong rope ; there must be no unnecessary splashing by dropping from the wall into the moat. Carefully, and with scarcely a creak to break the stillness, the aperture in the wall was made. The three stole forth. From the house-portion of the fortress, and from the cluster of huts beyond, came sounds of revelry and feasting. All around was stillness and semi-darkness.

" Luck is with us ! " whispered Gurth.

He fastened the leathern rope to Edwy's belt.

There was no difficulty in mounting the wall from the inner side. A moment more and the two brothers lay along the top. Edwy swung himself over. Swiftly Gurth lowered him. The water rose to his waist. He gave a sharp tug at the rope, and at the signal Gurth let it go. The lad struck swiftly out, and in a couple of moments was clambering up the opposite bank. He unfastened the rope, wound it into a coil and sent it skimming through the air and over the wall again. Halford picked it up.

" Now ! " cried Gurth, " quick, and I'll lower you. I can dive, and make but little noise."

Halford climbed up. The rope was fastened underneath his arms ; Gurth took off his helmet and mail corselet, both of which might prove serious impediments to him in his dive into the chilling waters, gave them to Halford, and the latter speedily joined Edwy on the bank. A clean, and as nearly as possible, noiseless plunge, a few swift, strong strokes, and Gurth, dripping from head to heel, stood with them.

He wrung the water from his hair.

" It must be a sharp run, my lord, or the weather will be our undoing," said the henchman.

" Off, then, at your fleetest pace."

But they were not to escape so easily. They had not given ten strides towards the river before Halford suddenly stopped running and threw himself flat on the sodden grass, dragging Edwy with him. In an instant Gurth was beside him. " What is it ? " he asked.

Before an answer could be given, the sound of voices smote upon the thane's ears. He raised his head and peered into the darkness. Two figures loomed dimly before him. They were advancing rapidly towards ap Morgan's stronghold, and the three unarmed and shivering Saxons lay directly in their path.

It was a perilous situation. To get up and run was to ensure instant detection ; there was no time to crawl sufficiently far to escape their eyes.

Had it not been for the fact that they had run with the fort for a dark, obliterating background to their movements, their first step from the walls must have betrayed them. This thought flashed through Gurth's mind. " Back to the moat ! as quickly as we can crawl," he whispered.

The idea was the lucky inspiration of a moment, and it was as quickly acted upon. Back they crawled, but the two men came on faster than they moved from them. They reached the bank, crawled down, and hid amongst the reeds that grew there.

Within a yard of them the two men passed, gaily chattering. They waited and listened until the porter had answered their summons, raised the small draw-bridge, admitted them, and lowered it again. Then they rose up cautiously, glanced carefully around, and struck off swiftly and silently, but at an angle to their former direction.

Unless they made a long detour this would carry them beyond the usual ford of the river. Halford asked whether the detour should be made, expressing an opinion against it himself, for any pursuit would certainly be aimed dead in that direction. Gurth agreed with him, and they made for another ford higher up stream, away from any beaten track, and unfortunately not connected with the Dean except by circuitous and seldom trodden pathways.

They reached the Wye without further mishap, just as the moon, bright and unclouded, rose over the trees. They waited until its beams fell clear across the swirling waters before they attempted the somewhat dangerous passage. Then they crossed, Edwy astride Halford's shoulders ; for the current was strong, and the water in places rose almost to Gurth's armpits.

At the moment when they stood, dripping but exultant, on the high bank of the Saxon shore, Orcar and his men went with a stealthy but swinging tread down the slope, making in a bee line for their late prison.

We will leave them on their march, and continue for a brief while longer to follow the fortunes of Gurth and his two companions.

" Now, Halford," said Gurth as they moved off into the shelter of the trees, " we must trust ourselves to thy guidance, for, to speak honestly, I am little better than one lost in this part of the Forest. Dost thou think we can reach home to-night ? "

" I do not think it wise to try, my lord, seeing that we are unarmed and soaked to the skin."

" What dost thou advise, then ? "

"That we stay here. There are caves in these rocks, and if we can find one snug and dry, we must grin at the thief hunger and wait for daylight."

They commenced their search for shelter at once. Halford, who had known the place well as a boy, found a roomy cavern in a side of the sandstone cliff away from the river. It contained large quantities of dried leaves which had drifted in, and some bracken. Halford had not forgotten the mysteries of woodcraft, and after some labour succeeded in kindling a fire and making up three comfortable beds. All three undressed, hung their clothes round the somewhat smoky fire, rolled themselves up in the heaps of leaves, and, in spite of hunger and cold, fell fast asleep.

Leaving them thus comfortably disposed, we will now concern ourselves with the expedition of Orcar.

Down the narrow paths in long files swept the Saxons, avoiding as much as possible the dry and crackling undergrowth. They debouched upon the plain, formed up in two compact bodies with narrow fronts, and, preceded by keen-eyed, silent scouts, set out upon the final stage of their march.

Half the distance had been quickly covered when one of the scouts came running back with the tidings that the enemy was on the alert. Hardly had Orcar heard his tale than another scout fell back upon the main bodies. He reported that a small body of the enemy was almost upon them, but advancing too rapidly to be really aware of their nearness.

In an instant every Saxon was prone and silent upon the ground. The Welshmen came on, to the number of seven or eight, almost at a run and heading directly for the ford. The darkness where they lay effectually hid the lurking foe until it was too late.

A sharp signal, a sudden rising up of a mass of

men from the earth, a brief struggle, hardly a cry, and the Welshmen lay in the tracks of the Saxons. Some were disarmed and bound ; a few who offered resistance were stretched out motionless and dead. The affair was over in a few moments, and the men moved on more swifty than before.

The scouts vanished again amidst the straggling trees and bushes, utilising every shadow. Orcar saw that a complete surprise was now out of the question ; still he hoped to catch his foe only partially prepared.

No more scouts returned, and as they neared the Welsh stronghold no great noise or commotion was discernible. They reached the foot of the slight slope upon which the fortress was raised, and within a hundred yards of the edge of the moat. As far as they could ascertain, they were undiscoverd. Orcar suspected a trap. Once again the men lay down, the scouts were now not a score of yards ahead. Orcar advanced to them, and at his orders they crawled to the top of the slope and carefully surveyed the inter-vening ground. A few men were busy about the gate and drawbridge, the former of which stood open, and the latter lowered ; a few of the Welsh, too, stood about on the walls. But there was no evidence of any expectation of an enemy.

Thinking that his presence on the Welsh side of the river was known, Orcar could hardly be anything else than supremely astonished. He went forward to examine the state of affairs himself. The spies had reported truly.

His plans were made in an instant. The prisoners he ordered to be gagged and stripped. They were

five in number, and five sturdy foresters soon stood
arrayed in their clothes, and armed with their weapons.
The whole body moved to within a yard of the top,
and spread out in a semicircle two deep. Then up
came the pretended messengers at a run. Still at
a run, and without a moment's hesitation, they made
straight for the gate.

The guard saw them, thought he recognised them,
wondered why they did not speak or shout some
greeting. But they came on as men blown with a
long race. He suspected nothing, until the foremost
runner thrust forth his spear, and he felt the point
grating past his ribs. Then he gave a wild yell of
pain and warning, and fell. As he reeled he thought
he saw a vision of an advancing wave of men ; he was
dead before he could learn that it was no vision, but
reality.

But the others at the gate, and the men on the wall
saw all, and heard all. Shouts and cries resounded
on all sides. A fierce struggle was already going on
at the gate. Orcar dashed for the drawbridge, and
reached it just as it creaked on the rise. One swing
of his sword, and the strained ropes were severed.
The gate was now at the mercy of him and his men.

But the ap Morgans came from their hold like bees
from their hive. They swarmed upon wall and tower,
and poured a death-dealing hail of spears and arrows
into the ever-thickening press of foemen on the bridge.
Orcar broke from the press and directed the long line
of his men to attack the spearmen and archers.

The mass of Welshmen on the inner side of the
gate was now as great as that of the Saxons on the

outer. It was a living ram battering upon a living wall. The besiegers had no scaling ladders with them, and the moat was deep, and the wall high. The living barrier must be broken away. Cut and thrust, scream and shout, the fight went on. Men fell wounded, dying, dead ; and a ghastly barrier was growing up between the furious combatants.

Again Orcar withdrew from the press for a moment to see how the battle went. Clearly it was not going in his favour as much as he had hoped and wished. His line of men was too exposed, and the light of the moon grew clearer and stronger. The Welshmen were numerous and well-protected, and they fought with the nimbleness and ferocity of mountain cats. The walls must be scaled.

" Into the moat, the biggest of you," shouted the thane.

A score of stalwart fellows plunged in at once. They swam to the wall. They felt for the bottom with their feet. With some of them the water rose to their necks. But they shouted to their companions on the bank to come on.

Another lot plunged in, glad to escape the monotony of being shot at from loophole and window. Up on the backs of their fellows they went. They stood on the shoulders, they stood on the upstretched hands. The pressure brought the mouths of some down to the level of the water, so that they gasped for breath.

But the top of the wall could now be reached, and with the activity of the squirrels of their Forest home, they swung themselves up. Some came headlong down again, pierced through with spear or arrow.

Those on the bank dragged them out, and others leapt in and were soon on the wall filling the empty places. Others swarmed in, and on, and over. The patient human stepping-stones came out from their icy bed, and joined vigorously in the fray at the gate in order to restore warmth.

The ap Morgans had not calculated on this sudden and daring storming of their walls. They were now attacked in front and in flank. They fell back from the gate, and the Saxons rushed in.

Along the inner side of the walls, and in the angles of the building the combat went on. But the defenders were losing heart, and the attacking party invigorated with triumph. Women and children were screaming and shrieking in the rear. Moreover, ap Morgan himself was disabled by a sword cut, and confounded at the unexpected onslaught, and the number of his enemies. In the confusion and the wintry moonlight he fancied them to be many more in number than they really were. He sounded a parley and begged for quarter.

Orcar commanded his men to stay their hands, and stepped forward to the wounded and puzzled chieftain.

" What is all this fighting for at the peaceable time of Christmas ? " asked the latter.

" Thou canst answer that best thyself," replied Orcar ; " the fault of it lies at thine own door."

" How can that pe ? I haf not taken cow or pig or pony from thy lands for many moons."

" Thou hast taken more than the land itself," cried Orcar. " What hast thou done with our lord, the thane of Wulf, and his brother, and his henchman ?

Set them free, and we will betake ourselves to the Dean again without delay."

The wily Celt raised his unwounded arm with a gesture of astonishment.

" Inteet ! " he exclaimed.   " We haf no thanes or lords with us.   The Wulf wass our guest, and we treated him well, and meant him no harm ; but he went from us this night."

" But not with thy blessing or goodwill," answered the Saxon leader, who now began to see through the whole business of the hasty scouts and the watchings from the wall.   " Didst thou not send after him ? " he continued.

" Am I a fool ? " snapped ap Morgan.

" Prove to me that they are gone."

The Welsh chief led the way to the hole in the wall. Orcar examined it, and chuckled softly.

" Good !   Now we will be thy guests until the return of all thy scouts.   Thou shalt show us the many kindnesses that the Wulf would not have of thee.   If he be harmed or roughly used, we will burn this place about thy ears."

So the thane Orcar abode that night with ap Morgan the younger.   And when morning dawned he set out again for the river, having first of all pledged the Welshman by a great oath that the young thane should be sent back with all speed and honour should he still be found on Welsh soil.

Ap Morgan sat in his hall nursing his wound and planning revenge.   He sent a messenger to his brother, and bethought himself of the Norman knight, Sir Gilbert de Tournay.

The Saxons returned to the ford and they that kept it. Nothing had been heard or seen of Gurth. Orcar was much perplexed, and in spite of the hole in the wall would have suspected the Welshman of playing him a trick, had it not happened that those who guarded the newly made causeway had seized two of the enemy's scouts and still held them prisoners. Upon examination of these the thane felt he could no longer doubt the story of the escape and the manner in which it had been effected. This assurance was agreeable, but the absence of any signs of the runaways was perplexing.

For some time they searched the river on both banks, but found no traces of the fugitives. Then Orcar determined to return to the castle of the Wulf, leaving a small body of men ambushed in the trees on the Saxon bank with instructions to wait there until the moon should be well up. He considered that by this time Gurth, if he were still at liberty, would attempt the passage of the river.

Let us return to our hero and see how it has fared with him since we left him sound asleep in his bed of leaves and bracken.

The night passed without accident. The fire at the mouth of the cave burned steadily and smokily. It served at the least to warm the damp and chilling air before it reached the sleepers, and it kept wolf and boar at a respectable and safe distance. And it attracted no human enemy to their resting-place.

The dawn came, wrapped in a cold and clammy mist. The sleepers stirred on their rude couches, and one by one they awoke. Halford brushed his leafy coverlet from him, went to the fire, raked it together and examined the clothes. He pronounced them dry, and they dressed quickly.

No sooner had they emerged into the open air than the claims of hunger began most vigorously to manifest themselves. How could they appease them? Some hours of difficult, tedious, and wary walking must elapse before they could hope to reach home. They were practically weaponless, and the way was dangerous. Food, too, was hardly procurable in these wilds without weapons. League after league, before and around them, stretched the wintry, almost pathless Forest. Truly their position, foresters as they were, was not an enviable one, for, except along the well-trodden ways and around their homes, the vast stretch of wild woodland was almost a sealed book to them.

But the most pressing claims must first receive attention. They proceeded to seek refreshment. Gurth and Edwy went down to the river and well soused their hands and faces in the stream; then, from a pool in the rocks where the water lay still and clear, they took a long, refreshing drink. Halford joined them, bringing with him a stout ash sapling which he had torn up from amongst the undergrowth. This Gurth trimmed with his dagger, and sharpened at one end to a long, keen point. It was then given to Edwy, who lay down on a ledge of rock about a foot above the water, and watched and waited to see if fortune should send a fish worth spearing within striking distance.

Gurth and Halford climbed to the top of the bank

again, and gathering a few stones, set off in different directions among the trees in the hope of knocking down a bird or two.

As a rule, pigeons and doves abounded in the Forest, and small birds would doubtless be plentiful enough along the margin of the river.

Necessity will steady the hand and direct the eye, and soon Gurth and Halford drew near to the cave again, the former carrying a pair of pigeons, and the latter a pigeon and a good plump blackbird. Here, at any rate, was a good breakfast, even if Edwy had caught nothing. This proved to be the case, for when he was called he came up empty-handed and crest-fallen from the water.

Leaving his young masters to pluck, spit, and roast the birds, Halford set off again, dagger in hand, to procure three good, stout sticks, which should serve not only for helping them along the ofttimes miry and swampy way, but also for defending them in case of attack by some prowling beast.

When he returned, furnished as he desired, he found the birds browning beautifully amongst the glowing embers and emitting a fragrance truly delightful to the nostrils of a hungry man. Without ceremony they all set to, and ate with an appetite begotten of safety after many perilous adventures, a long run, a long rest, and a sixteen hours' fast. The bones were picked, and hunger appeased for a while. Halford scrambled down the bank again, and came back with Gurth's helmet full of water.

"Now," said the young thane, "we will make up our fire again, and get us a meal we may eat upon the way, for, how long that way may prove to be, and what luck may meet us upon it, we cannot say. Look thou to the fire, Edwy, and Halford and I will look to the food."

The young lad rose to do his brother's bidding, but at the mouth of the cave he paused suddenly, and as suddenly darted in again.

"There is a boat making for the bank," he cried. "She hath four men in her, all well armed!"

Gurth crawled to the opening and peered forth. The men were plainly visible around the shoulder of rock which hid the cave.

The three Saxons looked anxiously at one another. Were they discovered? Gurth glanced at the fire. It no longer smoked; nothing was left but glowing embers. These could not betray them, for they could not be seen from below. They watched.

The boat glided between the rocks and lay half in and half out of the very pool from which they had taken their morning drink. Deliberately the men tied her up. Then they turned, and just as deliberately commenced to ascend the bank, carefully following the track the fugitives had made.

"They have tracked us," whispered Gurth.

"Even so!" replied Halford, "and they know we are unarmed."

In single file, stealthily and silently as cats, the Welshmen came on. As yet they had betrayed their presence by no sound. Equally silent were the three in the cave. Nothing broke the stillness save the rushing and swirling of the river, and the chirp of a few birds.

The leading man paused and took a short spear from his back.

Gurth slipped to the side of the cave and beckoned the others to follow him. They stood upright in the shadow, where they could not be seen except the intruder stood a full yard within the entrance.

" Do we fight, my lord Gurth ? "

" To the last gasp ! "

Halford set his grim jaws and edged nearer to the entrance.

" Give me thy dagger, my lord, and look thou to this fellow's arms when I seize him."

Gurth gave up the weapon. A slight crackling came from outside. Halford bent slightly forward with open hands. A head appeared. A pair of eyes peered in. They saw the fire and the remains of the breakfast—nothing else.

The fellow made a sign to his comrades. He crawled in, half raised himself from his stooping posture ; his eyes went for a moment to the ground. The glance was fatal. A fearful and instantaneous living vice gripped his throat. He was jerked in with a force that almost dislocated his neck. Another vice tightened on his arms. A moment more and his body was thrown aside. The whole thing was done so quickly that he saw nothing, and barely struggled. Another head appeared, and just as swiftly was it seized, and just as speedily it ceased to wag for ever.

" Now," cried Gurth, seizing a spear, " no more of this work ; we are man to man."

He dashed across the entrance. The on-coming Welshman came full tilt breast on to the thane's spear. Gurth hurled him backwards down the steep path. His body struck against the fourth assailant who was close at his heels. The latter reeled, seized a bush to save himself, and thus presented a mark which Halford instantly and fatally hit.

The two bodies went crashing pell-mell one over the other down the rocks. From a position, seemingly helpless, the three Saxons emerged without a scratch, and four wily foes found death at the end of an hour's patient watching and waiting.

But the idea of complete security was dispelled. The arms of the dead men were collected ; four spears, four good knives, a stout bow, and a sheaf of arrows were thus obtained.

The foraging arrangements underwent alteration. Edwy rebuilt the fire, but Halford set out, alone, in search of game. Gurth took the boat, rowed across the stream, mounted the opposite bank, and, spear in hand, kept careful and anxious watch against surprisal.

But nothing happened to disturb them. A good supply of food was cooked. Edwy's proposal that they should take the boat and row down to the main ford and path was both rejected on account of the dangers of the way, and also for fear that such an important loophole would be well-watched.

They sent the boat adrift down the stream, and about noon, well-armed and well-provisioned, set out for home.

CHAPTER IX.

NOW all these things had not happened in the Forest without some tidings of them coming to the ears of the knightly smith of Eadburga Street.

The first news came from one of Orcar's house-carles who had been sent at once to the city to learn what he could of the movements of de Tournay and his friends. Of de Tournay's movements, or abiding-place, nothing was known for some days. The city held him not, and spies reported him absent from his castle near to Mitcheldean.

Then came the snow, preventing further communication. But the Norman was busy ; and neither his greatest friend nor his greatest enemy could have divined the thoughts that chiefly occupied his mind. For the first few days they were almost all of Gurth and revenge. He held many councils with his Welsh friends. But one vision of the young Saxon thane gradually worked itself into exasperating prominence. It comprised the last scene in the chapter-house, and the angel of the vision was the beautiful and modest daughter of the smith. Soon her face was before him day and night. His allies from over the border were forgotten. Revenge took on another shape.

When the snowfall had ceased, but two days before the thaw commenced, he took four of his most trusted men-at-arms and set out for Gloucester. He entered in the evening, dispersed his men—who had received careful orders—betook himself to secluded lodgings, and remained for the most part indoors. No friend of our Saxon acquaintance knew of his presence in the city.

Meanwhile, his satellites watched the house of Sir John the Smith. The gentle Elgiva was dogged as she went hither and thither through the snow on her little errands of mercy.

Patience and perseverance in any cause, bad or good, meet with their reward. One night—the very one upon which three captives escaped—one most dear to all three of them was ensnared. Elgiva called upon her old pensioners in the abbey precincts. She had not called since the night of her meeting with the luckless Norman gallant, now gone to his account. The old couple had heard of the adventures, and Elgiva, nothing loth, had to answer many artless questions concerning the brave young Forest thane. She stayed later than she had intended, and this time there was the lurking foe, but no watchful friend.

Emerging from the low doorway she ran quickly along the path towards the Westgate Street, but no sooner had she got into the shadow of the wall than she was seized from behind, gagged, and hurried off by bypaths to a mean hut against the north-west wall of the city. There she was compelled to adopt the attire of a page, the four vile rascals giving her clearly to understand that unless she did so promptly, they would perform the office for her.

In less than an hour from the time of the seizure four men-at-arms and a page, all warmly wrapped up and hooded, rode quickly forest-wards from the Westgate. Had the warder been less occupied in the warming of his own chilled limbs, he might perhaps have noticed that the page sat his horse but awkwardly, that he was crying, and that his mouth and chin were enveloped in a thick wrap. And had he noticed all these things, he in all probability would have accounted for them on the score of the cutting wind which came howling across the half-frozen, swampy meadows.

Just before reaching Minsterworth the small cavalcade diverged from the roadway to a hut in the fields. This, by arrangement, was found empty ; but a fire burned on the earthen floor, and food and drink were discovered after a very short search. Here, cold, hungry, thirsty, in terror and in misery, Elgiva spent the long winter night.

The next morning one of the men prepared breakfast soon after daybreak. However, neither threats nor persuasions prevailed with their captive, who refused to take anything more than a cup of water from the neighbouring well.

As soon as practicable they set out again on their journey. As on the previous evening, they avoided every cluster of houses. Nearing Westbury-on-Severn, they struck off again into the open country, and, heading northwards, left Newnham some miles to

the west of them. Their aim was to strike a path
in the north-eastern border of the Forest, and then
go along the bridle path through Flaxley Wood to
Mitcheldean. By pushing on they hoped to be safely
housed at noon. But as the morning wore on the
rate of progress grew slower and slower. Elgiva was
so worn with fatigue as scarcely to be able to sit
her horse.

The wintry sun was almost at its highest when they
entered the dimness of the main belt of woodland.
The hollows in the pathway and in the glades were
knee-deep in slush and water. The escort grew
hungry and angry. They began to curse their luck,
their master, their trembling captive, and the whole
of the melancholy business. Twice they were startled
by the loud howls of the wolves on the rising ground
before them. Elgiva's terror increased tenfold. She
prayed earnestly for deliverance from all her dangers,
and her thoughts wandering homewards pictured her
parents in their misery and despair at her mysterious
disappearance. She wondered if they were following
her ; if they would reach her in time.

Then came thoughts of another. Where was Gurth ?
Was he yet a captive ? Was he in the hands of the
same people who had entrapped he ? Should she see
him ? Would they escape together ?

Despite the rough, uncertain, jolting way, despite
the rude oaths and grumblings around her, she fell
a-dreaming fitfully. First, she and Gurth were
prisoners. They met, and plotted, and escaped.
They wandered alone in the Forest for days. Gurth
made a bower for her each night in the trees,

and lit a fire to scare the wolves away. In the morning he left her for a little while and brought back food for the day; and she dressed and cooked it with her own hands. And they were never cold or wet or hungry—and always happy!

Her horse stumbled down a slippery bank. She roused from her dream; she was a prisoner still. Yet her whole body glowed warmly, and she found she was smiling. Then the sighing of the wind through the trees brought her another dream. She was a prisoner and alone. And her gaoler was the young Norman who had tried to kiss her. He was surrounded too by many of the scowling faces she had seen at the king's court. But a morning of deliverance came. The fierce war-cry of the " Wulf," as she had heard it at the supper in her father's hall, came ringing and echoing over and around the castle walls; and through the splintered gates and over the battlements came surging miners, apprentices, foresters, and in the forefront of all came Gurth, her father, Orcar, and the king! It was a glorious deliverance, for the first to reach her was Gurth, and he kissed her hand just as he did the night he accompanied her from the abbey.

She was not conscious of it, but her face was suffused with a burning blush, and tears stood in her eyes. She sighed. The dream faded slowly, and a third one, most wonderful of all, she thought, grew distinct and luminous in its place. Gurth and Edwy and Halford had escaped from their prison and were journeying joyfully home through the Forest. As she wound along the path with her captors, she caught sight of them as they crossed a narrow glade trudging gaily along and laughing at the difficulties of the way. She screamed out the young thane's name and called on him for help. With a rush and a wild shout all three came bursting across the open towards her. In a trice the four cowards with her were laid low in the mire. The three Saxons sprang on the horses, Gurth smiled, and whispered his joy to her. He took her bridle and——

An actual and fierce tug at the bridle nearly threw her from the saddle. A surly voice asked her with an oath why she did not attend more to her going? Did she wish to break her neck and get theirs broken too, after all the trouble they had had on her account?

The poor girl came back to the grim and dread reality, but she choked back the rising sobs and repressed the rush of tears. She felt faint and giddy, parched with thirst, and sick for lack of food; but her dreams had cheered her, and she determined to bear herself bravely and to trust to God and those who loved her so dearly for succour.

But a worse trial than all lay before her. She was to see some of those of whom she had dreamed, and yet be unable to call upon them for deliverance.

They had passed almost through Flaxley Wood, and were within a few miles of Mitcheldean, but it was more than an hour past noon. They came to a little stream, and she begged that she might alight for a moment and quench her thirst. This was granted, the more readily because the men were only too glad to do the same. All dismounted and led their horses through the trees to a higher part of the brook where the water ran more clearly.

Elgiva's request proved nothing less than a disaster. Scarcely had she dipped her hands into the welcome water than a stirring of the undergrowth and a confused sound of voices at no great distance attracted not only the attention of her companions, but her own. Instantly the fellows ran to their horses and forced them farther back into the trees, where they would be secure from observation. Three stayed beside them, but one returned to Elgiva and made her crouch in concealment with him behind a bush which grew at the water-side. Laying his mailed hand upon her shoulder, he told her that if she made any attempt to cry out, it would instantly tighten round her throat and maybe silence her voice for ever.

So, in stillness and with quickly beating hearts, they watched and waited. The sounds came nearer and clearer, and soon a straggling line of men appeared amongst the trees. Speech and dress proclaimed them Saxons and foresters. At their head marched one whom Elgiva quickly recognised as the thane Orcar. She started with excitement. The hand gripped her shoulder cruelly, and she became still as a statue again.

The path these men were pursuing branched off from the one the Normans were traversing a few moments before. Had they gone on, detection would have been inevitable.

When the band of Saxons reached the place where their pathway crossed the streamlet, they gathered into a group, and presently hallooed loudly, and then waited for a reply. This they did several times. Some of the men, too, wound repeated foresters' calls upon their horns. Everything pointed to the fact that they sought some lost friend in the Forest. Who could it be?

Elgiva knew of no lost one save herself. Could it be that they were seeking her? The same thought crossed her companion's mind. She knew that it did so, for the heavy hand was removed from her shoulder and placed across her mouth, with a roughness that brought the blood from her lips.

Fired by a sudden resolve to attract attention, she struggled to free herself, but the brutal fellow held her safely. One by one the Saxons straggled off along the narrow track and disappeared from view.

When the hapless captive saw her hope of rescue gone, she threw herself prone on the sodden ground and sobbed as if her heart were breaking. The day-dreams that had cheered her were proving a hollow mockery.

For some considerable time the Normans did not venture from their concealment. Then, one of their number ventured forth and followed the Saxons some distance along the path. When he returned and reported the coast clear, they mounted, and rode from the place as quickly as possible.

But more than an hour had been lost, and every step towards home brought them fresh evidences that, for some purpose or other, their enemies were abroad in force. This was disquieting to the spirits of the four hungry and much-hated rascals. To push on at all hazards was the only course open to them.

Two precautions, wise enough in themselves, they adopted; but these very precautions proved their ruin. To guard against the possibility of unwittingly falling into the hands of their enemies, one of their number rode some distance ahead, keeping a wary outlook; another detached himself and formed a rearguard, whilst the other two rode with Elgiva between them. They would willingly have abandoned her to whatever fate the Forest wilds had in store for her, only de Tournay's orders for her safe carrying to his castle were strict, and, moreover, they did not know what his ultimate purpose with her might be.

Further to minimise the risk of falling into an ambush, they forsook the more direct ways to Mitcheldean and travelled by circuitous tracks, tending to keep them in the denser woodland to the south and towards Ruardean. This rendered progress slower and more tedious, but it led them from all visible indications of an enemy's presence.

Now, the path pursued by Gurth and his two companions lay in a south-easterly direction from the river, and about midway between the two above-mentioned Forest settlements. And so, hopeless and heart-broken as Elgiva was, there was yet a chance of her third dream receiving some measure of fulfilment. In fact, Dame Fortune had administered cuffs enough, and was now in the mood for caresses.

The Normans had ridden for barely the space of half an hour from the time of their restarting, when they came to another small open space, where four ways met. One they were now upon; another was its continuation river-wards; a third went south to

Ruardean and beyond that to the castle of the Wulf; the fourth (and this was the one they purposed following) led to Mitcheldean.

Already the foremost horseman had turned into the northern path and was lost to view, and the two central ones were within a half-score yards of the crossing.

Suddenly, close ahead, from the river-ward path, there came a hearty burst of laughter, followed by a rushing and trampling among the bushes, and a hunting "halloo!"

So utterly unexpected was it, that the Normans instinctively reined in their horses and listened. Elgiva listened too, her heart palpitating wildly; for, strangely and unexpectedly as the sounds had come, they rang familiarly in her ears. A momentary prayer went from her soul that the sounds would come again.

Her prayer was answered before her escort had time to recover themselves. From a bush close at hand came another violent stumbling, a gruff exclamation, half angry, half amused, and a peal of boyish laughter. Before a hand could be put forth to prevent her, she had urged her horse forward with a bound, and "Halford! Edwy! Gurth! my lord Gurth! help me! help me!" burst wildly from her lips. She threw back her hood, and let her hair stream forth in the wind, so that they might the more readily recognise her in her strange disguise.

But nothing more than her piteous cry was needed. As one, the three Saxons sprang into the pathway before her, and in a moment more Edwy's hand was on her bridle. The Normans hearing so many names called, and fearing another large company, hesitated for a moment as to what they should do. However, on recognising the two lads, they hesitated no longer but dashed forward to recover their prey.

Too late, however. The pause, momentary as it was, was their undoing. Gurth had an arrow ready fitted to the bow he carried when he emerged from the bushes. Recognising in a flash Elgiva's imploring face, and the hated livery of de Tournay, he raised his weapon, and the arrow sped through the heart of the foremost foe, who dropped the reins convulsively and fell all of a heap to the ground. The other fared no better, for even Edwy's boyish heart throbbed with fury at his beloved playmate's degradation. He let go the bridle, dived under the horse's belly and from a distance of barely six paces hurled a spear full at the fellow's face, the Norman's attention at the moment being concentrated upon Halford, who was rushing forward, spear in hand, to attack him. Edwy's missile hit its mark, making an ugly wound in the fellow's cheek.

With a yell of pain he turned his horse to ride down the youngster, but Edwy, with another quick dive, was back to his former position, and in another moment the Norman fell, Halford's spear in his shoulder, and an arrow of Gurth's in his lungs. The hindmost horseman, who was hastening forward, seeing the fate of his companions, swerved round into the shelter of the trees, and made for home. The foremost one, who was returning at the noise of the shouting and fighting, on seeing the other making off at such a headlong pace, turned his horse again and dashed off along the pathway.

So our heroes were once again masters of the field, with two good horses for spoil, and the rescue of a priceless captive to make their joy and gratification inexpressible.

Poor Elgiva! No sooner had they lifted her from her horse than, overcome with excitement, terror, joy, fatigue, and hunger, she went off into so dead a faint that the lads were more concerned than they had been at her appearance as the prisoner of the Normans. But Halford took her tenderly in his arms and carried her from the gruesome spot to a spring that bubbled up at a short distance off. Here she revived, and partook of the provisions the three had with them. This so cheered her, that smiles and blushes soon began to contend for the possession of her pretty face.

Without a moment's unnecessary delay they set off again, Gurth, Edwy, and Elgiva riding, and Halford striding along just ahead. Here was her dream fulfilled ; and she felt so happy that she could have gone through it all again if only it might have so delightful an ending.

Edwy rallied her on her appearance, and called her his "pretty brother." Gurth laughingly begged that he might become "esquire" to so lovely and all-conquering a "knight," and vowed that no evil thing could live within the arrowy glances of her eyes. The happy maiden bore it all very demurely, and commanded her "squire" to lead her steed by the bridle. This he did, for in her dream Gurth had done so.

Then the boys begged for an account of her adventures, and these she related to them as they rode along the way. How their blood boiled as they listened! And what deep and solemn vows of vengeance they took. Halford swore that he would return at once to Gloucester and make another axe, with which to cleave de Tournay's skull.

Then Elgiva enquired the cause of the laughter which had attracted their attention to them.

"Oh!" said Gurth, "a young boar that had strayed away from its fellow piggies found itself filled with a strange love for Halford. It trotted after him and alongside of him, sniffing and grunting, and amusing itself by getting entangled in his legs."

"It was strange for the wild thing to behave so," said Halford solemnly, "and when I get home I shall thank God for a miracle."

"And I will join in your thanksgiving," added Elgiva.

Chatting away, sometimes seriously, sometimes gaily, the little company rode along, and soon tower and gable and battlement peeped through the rapidly thinning trees, and home stood out to welcome them.

What a shout they raised when the loved and familiar scene burst upon them ! It rang through the glade and startled the watchman on his tower. Men flocked to the gate, recognised their young lord, and yelled out wild huzzas of welcome ; the younger bloods ran like forest deer to welcome them. Halford squared his mighty shoulders and strode on, a giant

refreshed.   The lads would have spurred on their
horses and have gone forward at the gallop, but that
they feared to overtax Elgiva's sorely tried strength.
She, awakening to the sense of her strange position,
quickly drew a cloak around her, and the vociferating
Saxons in the pauses between their joyous "hurrahs!"
wondered concerning the Norman page their young
lord brought back with him.   They crowded round
the horses, they crowded round Halford, pressing him
with questions.

Orcar and the Lady of the Dean, hearing the joyous
tumult, guessed the happy cause, and came forth to
the outer gate to welcome the lost ones.   What
embraces there were! and what tears of joy!   Again
and again the shouts went up, and the Forest welkin
rang, echoed, and re-echoed with cries of "A Wulf!
A Wulf!"

Gurth whispered to his mother concerning Elgiva;
but when the kindly dame turned to greet her, she
was nowhere to be seen.   The maiden had slipped
to little Editha's side, whispered who she was, and
the two had stolen off unnoticed to the women's
apartments.

At once, messengers, well-armed and well-mounted,
were dispatched to tell the smith of his daughter's
safety, and preparations were soon afoot for mighty
feastings and rejoicings.

Sir John, bursting with mingled sorrow and anger,
was met with on the Forest border.   Posthaste, he
and the messengers came to the Dean, whilst his band
of smiths and apprentices went back to Gloucester
to tell the good tidings to Dame Alicia.

The banquet was spread, and the board duly swept of its good things. Halford was appointed the "skald" of the evening, and, nothing loth, he told with point and effect the story of their adventures. The horns of mead circulated swiftly, and toasts were drunk with acclamation. And one bold fellow brought the enthusiasm to its topmost height, by calling on all to drink "love and wassail" to their young lord and the beautiful maiden who sat blushing at his mother's side.

CHAPTER X.

ON the morning following the abduction of Elgiva there was great stir amongst the citizens of Gloucester. Sir John's loss was soon made known. East, west, north, and south search was made. Every nook and alley was explored, every suspicious character straitly questioned ; but nothing of importance was gleaned. The warders, one and all, declared that no maiden had quitted the city by the gates, and that she had quitted it by the walls was not to be thought of.

De Tournay showed himself frequently in the narrow streets of the city during the morning. He publicly condoled with the smith upon his sad and unaccountable loss, and much as Sir John mistrusted him, it seemed unjust to harbour suspicion against him.

But towards noon the Norman left the city at the western gate, accompanied by a small escort lent him by a city friend. News of this was brought to the smith, and it so happened that the worthy craftsman knew that de Tournay on his recent entrance into Gloucester was accompanied by his own men-at-arms. Enquiries within the walls failed to find any trace of them now, but several could tell of four men-at-arms

135   9

and a page who had left the city late the previous evening. Upon second thoughts one man was prepared to swear that they wore the de Tournay livery.

Such evidence, flimsy as it was, was quite sufficient for the astute and grief-stricken smith. He assembled the sturdiest of his workmen and apprentices, armed them to the teeth, and, in the company of several indignant fellow-citizens, he set out for the Norman's castle. How he fared on the way we know already. We have left him rejoicing at the Dean, drinking mead at the board of his liege lord, and, perchance, dreaming that his sweet maid may some day greet him, proud and happy in her high dignity, mistress of the house of Wulf.

Let us then leave him to his thoughts, and go with the baffled de Tournay to his stronghold.

The Norman rode at a great pace as soon as the walls of the city had sunk out of sight behind him. His brow was gloomy and his mind was torn by conflicting thoughts. He was but ill-satisfied with his late proceedings. As a rule he was not squeamish about his actions, and not accustomed to remorse, even when women were the sufferers. But the sweetness and purity of Elgiva's face haunted him. He half wished that he had not molested her; he found himself wishing wholly that he had met her under happier circumstances. Her winsome image had stolen into his heart and brain, and he ground his teeth in bitterness as he thought how she must hate him for the degradation he had put upon her. He vowed mentally that he would hang the whole of her escort if he found they had treated her roughly.

Then he began to shape out some plan of action that he might follow. He knew he had gone too far to retreat, and moreover, to restore her to her father was, possibly, to hand her over to his hated and hitherto triumphant foe, the young Saxon thane. He would hold fast to so precious a prize; and to do this he must find, at least for a time, some place of hiding and safety. Such a place might not easily be found in England, for de Tournay had already discovered that the arm of the king's power was long; and he did not wish to be found among the king's enemies.

His plan resolved itself as follows :—Firstly, to get to Mitcheldean as speedily as possible, and carry Elgiva away from thence in time to prevent her presence there becoming known. Secondly, to fly to his Norman home over the sea, and there either woo or compel the Saxon maiden to become his wife. Thirdly, to return in the end to the Forest, claim the alliance of Sir John, use his wife as a means to win some of the vassals of the house of Wulf from their allegiance, and, finally, by fraud and force to break down the power of his rival.

To the mind of de Tournay it was a goodly scheme and a feasible one. His mind felt settled and easy, and on his arrival before his castle he brought the warder to the gate by a stirring blast.

" Is Bertrand within ? " he asked of a servitor as he dismounted in the courtyard.

" He arrived a few minutes ago," was the reply.

" Good ! " ejaculated the knight.

The man made no reply, but he thought to himself that it was not " good." However, he kept his opinion

for he had no desire to bear the first brunt of his
master's anger.   De Tournay entered his hall with a
light step.

" Send Bertrand to me instantly ! " he commanded.
The seneschal disappeared.   The knight sat down in
a chair and gave himself up for a few moments to
pleasing fancies.   Bertrand entered.   He was the
soldier who had had charge of Elgiva.

De Tournay glanced up.   He saw that the man he
wanted stood before him, but he was too preoccupied
to notice the look of utter discomfort and dismay
which overspread the fellow's counntenance.

" Where hast thou placed the maiden ? " he asked.

No answer.

De Tournay looked up impatiently.   The hangdog
expression on Bertrand's face alarmed him.

" Hast thou harmed her ? " he demanded fiercely.

" She hath escaped ! "

The knight jumped to his feet.

" She hath,—what ? "

" We were waylaid by the Saxon hogs, and the
maiden was taken from us."

" And thou art here to tell me ? "

" I had no thought she was deemed of so much
value."

" Thou shalt find that thy life, and the lives of thy
three fellow-cowards just balance her safety," cried
de Tournay with a fearful oath.   " Ye shall hang,
the whole pack of ye ! "

" Thou wilt need sharper scent than the wolves
to find half the hanging matter then," muttered the
fellow surlily.

" What dost thou mean ? "

" My brother and Geoffrey are dead, shot through the heart."

De Tournay bit his lip and hesitated for a moment ; then he flung himself into his chair again.

" Tell thy tale from the beginning," he exclaimed.

The soldier shifted his position, fumbled his sword-hilt uneasily with his left hand, and began :

" We did all in the city and on the night according to thy directions, and no man saw us. This morning the maiden was weak, and would take no food. We rode slowly, else she had fallen from her horse and broken her neck. We lost time. The Saxons were abroad in force. We narrowly escaped from riding into an ambush of three score of them. We stayed in hiding, and when we moved forward I sent one man ahead, rode behind as guard myself, and set the maiden between with my brother and Geoffrey. At a turning in the path the three were set upon by a band led by the thane of Wulf and the giant fellow who rode with him from Gloucester. As I told thee, the two were shot dead. I thought it better to preserve a life for thee and bring thee tidings than to give myself to the wolves for no purpose."

During this laconic and surly recital the knight's face underwent many rapid changes of expression. At the mention of Gurth he glanced at Bertrand with a malicious leer.

" A clumsy string of lies," he said. " The thane of Wulf is a prisoner in Wales, or all Welshmen are liars."

" The thane of Wulf is drinking thy maiden's

health at his den in the Dean," answered the soldier bitterly.

"Thou art not careful of thy health," said de Tournay meaningly.

"My brother is a supper for the wolves, because a Saxon maiden hath blue eyes." The rough fellow's eyes were moist with tears.

De Tournay understood him.

"I believe thy tale; the Welshman hath played me false; we will hang those rascals of his who are with us instead of thee. Take men and find thy brother's body. Bring it hither that the priest may bury him as good man and true. After that I will help thee to thy revenge."

Bertrand left the room, and a few minutes afterwards rode forth into the Forest.

For a while his master sat motionless. He had reined in his anger and bitter disappointment only with a great effort. He tried to consider the matter calmly, but his passions seethed and bubbled inwardly like a fiery mountain. At length the volcano burst. He paced to and fro the room, restless as a caged and famished tiger. He muttered awful imprecations upon the heads of all concerned, not even sparing himself. His hatred of Gurth grew tenfold in an hour, and in keeping with it grew a mad yearning for Elgiva, and a fierce determination to possess her in spite of all.

The time flew by, but no one came to him. Every soul in the castle knew what had happened to its lord and master, and all wisely kept aloof.

Bertrand returned. The knight went into the courtyard and viewed the dead bodies of his retainers. In the breast of one an arrow still remained. He plucked it out, doubly red in the last rays of the winter sun.

"This is no Saxon arrow!" he cried abruptly. "That fox ap Morgan hath played me false indeed. By Heaven! some of his brood shall dangle in the starlight before the sun rise again. Guard every exit ; and go thou, Bertrand, and place them in hold thyself!"

The men sprang to do his bidding. Jabbering excitedly in broken English, protesting, threatening, the late escort of de Tournay were hustled into the freezing cells, and the great doors closed upon them. Bertrand settled grimly to his task of preparing a set of stout halters. His master breathed more freely. The work of revenge was commencing with a bold flourish. The outlook was more promising.

Twilight deepened amid the bustle of great preparations. Just when the brightest stars began to make apparent their presence in the sky, Bertrand announced that the halters were finished and already dangling from the castle walls in expectation of their tenants. De Tournay commanded the Welshmen to be led forth, and the whole body of retainers and servitors to be assembled.

The appearance of the prisoners was the signal for a perfect babel of expostulation. Seeing the knight standing in the courtyard, they forced their way towards him, and with one voice demanded an explanation of his infamous conduct.

"That you shall have," said he, "and a short shrift afterwards. Your fox of a chieftain hath played the traitor, set free mine enemies and armed them to slay my men; here lies the evidence. Look you at this arrow; it was shot from ambush by the thane of Wulf!"

The Welshmen gazed in consternation at the stiff cold bodies and the blood-stained weapon. They stood dumbfounded. Angry corroboration of the knight's words was stamped on every scowling face around them.

They recovered their power of speech with a string of voluble curses against the man who had played them so foul and deadly a trick. Then eager for life and revenge, they turned to de Tournay, and offered if he would set them free to take a solemn oath to avenge this treacherous trick to themselves and him. They pleaded their own innocence and ignorance.

The Norman was inclined to listen to their words, but Bertrand and the men clamoured for instant execution. De Tournay needed the unfaltering good-will of his villains, so he gave way to them.

"No!" cried he, "I trusted your chief. He has proved false; I will trust a Welshman no more. Hang you shall; so look to the priest."

Seeing that their cause was hopeless, the condemned men turned to the priest in order to gain time and a little spiritual consolation. Stillness reigned, save for the sighing of the wind in the forest and the murmurs of the priest. The ropes swayed to and fro in the breeze, and one by one the stars grew brighter.

Suddenly, from the foot of the wooded hill on which the castle stood, there came the faint sound of a bugle blast; a moment's silence, and it was followed by a second. The attention of every one was arrested, and the shadow of death lifted a little from the souls of the prisoners. The voice of the priest was hushed, and every ear was strained to catch a recurrence of the sounds. A few moments passed and they came again, clearer and stronger.

De Tournay turned to the warder. "Dost thou recognise the calls?"

"I do not, Sir Knight!"

The assemblage looked perplexed.

A third time the sounds rang out through the night. The men, whoever they were, were rapidly approaching.

A guilty man suspects all things. And, moreover, the Norman felt himself now to be surrounded by secret and open foes.

"Take these men away! Remove those ropes! Every man to his place at the walls!" he ordered sharply.

The Welshmen were hurried away again to dungeons and darkness. Every watcher on the walls strained sight and hearing to penetrate the secret of the night. There were footfalls on the path at the hill-top, then two faint, moving shapes on horseback; a pause, and a shrill bugle call burst forth within a hundred yards of the drawbridge.

"Who rides there?" shouted the sentinel from the tower above the gate.

"Friends to the Norman, and messengers from Morgan ap Morgan!" was the ready response.

De Tournay himself advanced to the walls.

"Ye are welcome, my friends!" he cried, "and shall be admitted with all speed."

He turned to Bertrand. "Two more goodly lengths of stout hemp; these fools come to their hanging like moths to a candle!"

The man-at-arms vanished in the darkness. Meanwhile, the drawbridge was lowered and the castle gates thrown open.

The messengers rode quickly in, dismounted, and came hurriedly towards de Tournay. The flickering torchlight half disclosed the cruel sneer on his lips. But the newcomers paid scant attention to his features; they proceeded to business with all dispatch. The foremost one dropped on one knee, rose again, and began:

"Sir Knight, we are come to thee in great haste, and with ill tidings. Yesternight the Saxon chief Orcar crossed the river and came upon us with a great force. We were unprepared, and many of our men were out seeking the thane of Wulf, who had broken prison and escaped us. The Saxons forced our gates, but withdrew when we showed them that their friends were no longer in our keeping. They kept the fords all night, and keep them still, thinking the young thane hath not escaped from our side. But we have tracked them across the Wye, found their resting-place last night, and the bodies of three of our countrymen who were slain in an attempt to take them again. The Morgan ap Morgan sends greetings, and would fain learn your mind and purpose in this matter. He will be with you in all you may choose to do."

De Tournay listened to the recital in astonishment. The messenger had every air of sincerity, and his story was plausible ; but the Norman's suspicions were not easily lulled. He pointed to the two corpses in the courtyard and took the tell-tale arrow in his hand.

"These, my men, were slain to-day with weapons of yours. I have held your chief a traitor. Had you arrived a little later, you would have found some of your friends dangling from these walls. You are my prisoners until such time as I have proof of the truth of your words."

The messengers looked blank, but the spokesman quickly recovered himself. He whispered to his companion in Welsh. Then he threw his spear and dagger to the ground.

"So be it!" he exclaimed. "To-morrow you shall find us true men."

"I shall be glad to do so!" answered de Tournay ; and he spoke sincerely.

The messengers were sent to join their countrymen, and the hanging was postponed. Later in the evening they were removed to more comfortable quarters, and a goodly repast placed before them.

Sir Gilbert de Tournay passed a sleepless night.

Very early in the morning a servitor was sent to make enquiries in Mitcheldean, and two spies were sent to haunt the vicinity of Gurth's castle. They returned with ample confirmation of the previous night's news.

The Welshmen were released and ample explanation and apology made. Reconciliation was sealed by an ostentatious feast ; and at the feast the Norman agreed to the terms of a strict alliance. Ap Morgan's men then set out for home, and de Tournay was left to mature his plans. After the evening meal he spoke to his men as to his desires and purposes. His two chief ends and aims were the death of Gurth and the recapture of Elgiva.

To stimulate his followers on to the effecting of these and a few subordinate ones, he offered some substantial rewards. To the man who should succeed in slaying the redoubtable Halford he promised five golden crowns ; to the one who should kill Edwy or Orcar either in fight or ambush, ten crowns ; to the slayer of Gurth one hundred crowns ; and to those who should bring Elgiva to him unharmed, fifty crowns apiece, and an allotment of land.

These were extravagant bribes to a body of about two hundred hardened, reckless rascals, and perhaps fulfilment was never intended ; but they showed the deadly purpose of the Norman, and whetted the zeal of every follower.

Meanwhile, those most concerned by these matters knew nought of them. The days sped along swiftly and merrily at the great castle in the Dean, and little of any moment was happening there save that Love was weaving a net of golden meshes, and Gurth and Elgiva were getting hopelessly but happily entangled therein. Watchful foes lurked around them, but so secret were they that their presence was never suspected.

But a day came when the lurking serpents essayed a sting.

Our gallant young thane and the maid of his heart had wandered off alone into the denser woodland. During the ramble Gurth spied a glorious bunch of mistletoe growing on a low branch of a spreading oak. With a merry whisper to his blushing companion he rushed off to secure the prize. Elgiva followed slowly.

Gurth was already crawling along the bare and twisted limb when she halted beneath it. Busy as she was with her own tumultuous thoughts, yet she caught the sound of a faint rustling in some bushes to the left. Recent dangers and experiences had made a wary woman of the once unsuspecting girl. She turned her eyes but not her head in the direction.

A hand was slowly parting the twigs, another hand was holding a bow already half-strung ; a pair of eager eyes were intently following every movement in the tree.

The girl's heart stood still with terror ; she saw the whole plot in an instant. At present Gurth was comparatively safe, for the other branches so screened him that the concealed assassin could not take a sure aim. But this protection would not be his a moment longer ; he had secured the coveted plant and was preparing to descend. In the impulse of the moment Elgiva sought to keep him there.

"Gurth!" she cried excitedly, "what is that over your head?" She pointed in the direction above, and towards the concealed ruffian, hoping her lover might see him.

Gurth struggled to his feet in order to look. The move was a false one, for it exposed his full length to the enemy. With a pang of agony the girl saw it, and saw the murderous bow raised. But even then she saved him.

"Never mind, Gurth!" she called quickly; "quick! quick! down and kiss me!"

The unexpected words and strange tone startled Gurth. In a moment he swung himself to the ground within a yard of her. Simultaneously the bow twanged, but Elgiva springing forward and clasping him to her breast, the arrow intended for his heart found lodgment in her arm.

Gurth unloosed himself, and with a harsh shout of rage dashed towards the bushes, unsheathing his dagger as he ran. The fellow was hurriedly endeavouring to fix another arrow, but seeing the young thane—whom he looked upon as the author of the deaths of so many of his fellow-rascals—rushing so impetuously towards him, he suddenly lost nerve, and, throwing down his weapons, scuttled off for his life.

Gurth as quickly seized them, and continued the headlong pursuit, shouting as he ran, "Help ho! A Wulf! A Wulf!"

These cries added wings to the flying miscreant, so Gurth, mindful of Elgiva, sent the arrow whizzing after him, and returned to the oak tree.

There he found the brave-hearted girl pluckily endeavouring not to faint from pain, so he took her in his arms, and with many a tender caress and sweet admiring word bore her swiftly home again.

Gurth returned that afternoon to the Forest; the bunch of mistletoe had been forgotten. He found it, and some of Elgiva's blood had stained a berry red. He took it home, hung it above her couch, and kissed her over and over again.

CHAPTER XI.

THE tidings of the attempt upon Gurth's life, and the wounding of Elgiva, spread through the Forest like a fire. Men's blood rose to fever heat, and feud to the death with de Tournay was everywhere proclaimed. The Saxon leaders saw that a general and deadly struggle was inevitable, and they made preparations accordingly.

As warden of the Forest, Gurth sent a messenger to de Tournay commanding him to deliver to justice the abductors of Elgiva and the miscreants who had made attempts on his own life. The answer was a sneer of defiance. The young thane therefore made arrangements to enforce his authority. He issued a proclamation calling upon all loyal subjects of the king and vassals of the house of Wulf to be in readiness to follow his banner. The foresters received the summons with joy; and, pending the commencement of hostilities on a larger scale, they were not slow to make reprisals. The wolves quarrelled over more than one Norman carcass during the bleak nights of January, and Norman marauders became as scarce as butterflies amidst the trees.

But the Norman's plans were more matured than the

149

Saxon ones. De Tournay's arrangements were almost completed before the outrage in the woodland startled the Saxons to the making of theirs in earnest.

One morning in the earliest days of February, news came that the ap Morgans to the number of five hundred were assembling on the banks of the Wye, below Ross, and that a Norman force had gone from de Tournay's stronghold to hold the English end of the ford against surprise and thus afford them an unmolested passage. The tables were unexpectedly turned, and the Saxons were to be the besieged and not the besiegers.

Instant action was necessary, and instant action was taken. From all outlying places the foresters were called in. The miners of Cinderford entrenched themselves, the good folks of Littledean did likewise. Orcar departed at once from the castle and betook himself to Newnham. He saw to the defences of his house, gathered in his fisherfolk, his swineherds, and prepared himself either for a siege or for skirmishing movements in the Forest.

He scarcely anticipated any attack upon himself, for he knew that two such oddly assorted allies as ap Morgan and de Tournay were hardly likely to hold together long enough for a very extensive series of operations. However much the Norman might desire a systematic and slow method, such a proceeding was too much against Welsh custom to be acceptable to his friends. There would be some harrying and robbing along the line of march, but the old thane reckoned upon a swift movement and a speedy investment of the castle in the Dean.

His surmise proved correct. Leaving Cinderford and Littledean almost unmolested, the enemy, some seven or eight hundred strong, moved rapidly forward. By noon the Saxon ring of outposts began to close in upon the castle. An hour later the enemy came through the surrounding belt of trees ; they were in three columns and headed by the two Welsh chieftains and the Norman knight. Just out of bowshot from the castle they halted.

The Saxons disappeared behind their walls, and the drawbridge was raised. A pause ensued, as though each party awaited some message or formal demand from the other. But the castle gates remained closed, and no foeman advanced to the ramparts.

Gurth and Sir John, who commanded with him, were prepared, and had no desire to waste time in empty and fruitless preliminaries. Great though the odds were against them they felt confident of victory ; too much that was dear to them lay in the shelter of the walls for an enemy to be permitted to scale them.

The besiegers prepared for an assault. With the exception of an advanced guard of Norman bowmen, all disappeared again amidst the trees.

For the space of nearly an hour, the besieged Saxons heard nothing save the ringing of axes and the hissing of saws. Evidently Norman method and Celtic recklessness were to be combined in the coming attack ; it would be a hot one. They braced themselves to resist it.

The stir amongst the enemy increased, and there was a great flitting in and out amongst the trees.

10

Men struggled forward under the burden of great boughs and branches, which they laid down in long rows upon the brown, leaf-strewn turf.

Presently the bugles rang out, and the voices of the leaders called the men into the line of attack. When all was ready they came forward with a quick, swinging stride. In the forefront marched a long line of men, bearing the bushy branches and limbs of trees. These formed an almost perfect screen for the line of archers behind; whilst rearmost of all came a further line of pikemen and spearmen. The Saxons beheld with some feelings of trepidation the quick on-coming of this formidable array.

When within a score of yards of the walls the attacking party halted, and for a few moments the bowmen poured in a perfect hail of arrows from the shelter of their trellis-like rampart. From every loophole and coign of vantage the Saxons replied, and their shooting proved more damaging than the enemy had anticipated; for, acting under the orders of Sir John, the men aimed just above the line of attack, and so wrought considerable havoc amongst the pikemen.

Upon this, the enemy closed up his ranks. Another flight of arrows streamed in black streaks through the air, and, as they sped on their errand of destruction, the whole line started rapidly forward, the ends curving in to embrace the walls as they dashed on.

Hitherto an almost complete silence had been observed by the besiegers, but now yells of defiance, taunts, and hoarse battle-cries burst from them as they ran. Into the moat were hurled the boughs

"THE WHOLE LINE STARTED RAPIDLY FORWARD." [*p.* 152.

and beams, churning up the water, but sinking under the weight of other beams, and the men who plunged in finding a foothold upon them. Near to the gate the moat was almost filled up.

Sticking their short, stout-hafted spears into the crevices of the stoned-faced earthen rampart, the Welshmen clambered up like cats, and from the margin of the encircling water the archers kept up the hurricane of missile attack upon every defender who showed himself. And show themselves they did and that right valiantly, else had the castle of Wulf been taken in a trice.

They hurled down huge stones upon the foemen, crushing their limbs and pinning their bodies beneath the icy waters, where they struggled frantically to escape from death. They thrust them back from the walls with long spears ; and their own bowmen sent many an opposing " bender of the stout yew " toppling head foremost among his fellows in the moat, his body transfixed with an arrow.

Hither and thither along the line of defence darted Gurth and the doughty smith, encouraging, fighting, urging, commanding. Grimly the besiegers stuck to their work, and grimly the besieged stuck to theirs ; no foemen had yet maintained a moment's footing on the top of the wall.

The first wild burst of attack had almost spent itself, and the Welshmen, finding their numbers and onset were not invincible, began to slacken their efforts. But de Tournay had reckoned on this critical moment and was awaiting it, occupying himself in the meanwhile by directing the assault. He rose instantly to the occasion, rallied the laggards, and, at the head of a picked body of well-armed and well-armoured followers, led on the rush himself, directing his efforts to the angle of the wall flanking the gateway.

The movement was almost a success. It would have been a complete one, had not Gurth paid a close and almost unswerving attention to his chiefest and most hated foe. He saw the attack and met it by similar tactics. A reserve was stationed at the inner gate under the command of Halford. These now leapt to the walls, fresh and eager for the fray. There was a wild whirl of fight for a few moments, and the Normans were beaten back. Three of their number got within the rampart, but they never lived to boast of their deed; no quarter was asked, and none given.

The victory for the time being lay with the house of Wulf, and the besiegers drew off to a safe distance. They left half a hundred of dead behind them, and they carried off an almost equal number of wounded. Inside the walls less than two score needed the services of either surgeon or sexton. But the numbers still available outside the castle were more than treble the numbers within; and the enemy knew it, and would come again to the attack when they were breathed.

Gurth and Sir John made preparations to receive them. Under cover of a strong body of archers on the wall, a party was sent to clear the moat. The dead bodies of the enemy were left on the bank, but the timber was brought within the walls, where it was placed in readiness for missile purposes when the enemy should advance again.

The afternoon wore away, and night closed in dark and starless, but hostilities were not renewed. Watchfires gleamed out on tower and battlement, and an answering line of flame flared along the edge of the trees.

The Saxons sat down to supper, an anxious but not a silent party. Tongues wagged fast and furious ; Halford and some others constituted themselves gleemen. The "Song of the Wulf" rang out loudly and fiercely as ever, and many a ballad was roared recounting some Forest victory over the nimble and implacable enemy across the Wye.

The beautiful Lady of the Dean sat at the board, proud, smiling and confident. With looks and voice she cheered the spirits of her men, and Elgiva, now rosy with excitement, now pale with apprehension, sat at her side. The young thane and the old smith took counsel of one another in a low voice.

Presently Gurth rose to his feet, and the babel around him ceased.

"Three men," cried he, "who can, without fail, find Newnham, Littledean, and Cinderford in the dark !"

There was an eager leaping to feet all round the table. After a careful scrutiny four of the volunteers were chosen. Gurth then went on to explain their errand.

"Our foes," said he, "will not attack us to-night in this darkness ; they are strong, full of hope, and will await the dawn. They outnumber us greatly, but the Wulf yields up his den to no pack of mongrel dogs, however many they be. We shall entrap them all if our night-runners carry truly. They are, severally, to bid the men of Cinderford, of Littledean, and the brave and worthy thane of Newnham to march hither with the daylight. They shall ambush themselves until the din of battle gives them their signal. Then they shall close in around us. We will break out from our walls, and these sneaking curs who snap and snarl at us from behind those bushes shall know what it is to feel our teeth in the open ! "

This spirited harangue was cheered to the echo again and again. All applauded the young thane's purpose, and all envied those chosen to act such a foremost part in the enterprise.

The runners were dispatched ; one to Cinderford, one to Littledean, but two to Newnham, for the way was long and dangerous. The ladies went back to their attendance upon the wounded, the men sought rest in slumber, and Gurth and Sir John saw to the arrangement of the night-watches.

Meanwhile their adversaries were not idle, and whilst the men sang, caroused, and boasted, the leaders planned the scheme of the next day's operations. The method of advance under the shelter of a screen of boughs was again to be adopted ; but, in addition, long, rough, heavy, but serviceable ladders were to be constructed. These were intended to span the moat and reach to the top of the ramparts ; their very weight would ensure their fixity. Branches of pine, knotted and resinous, heaps of brushwood were also to be collected, for it was intended to fire the gates and drawbridge. Furthermore, to intimidate the surrounding foresters from attempting attacks in the rear, de Tournay had arranged for a daydawn raid upon Cinderford. This, he anticipated, would effectually cow Littledean. Orcar, unaided, he did not fear greatly, and he hoped the castle of Wulf would be in his hands before that grim old warrior could advance to its relief.

The night deepened, and save for the calls of the sentinels and the cries of the wild and startled creatures of the Forest, silence stole over all.

Castle and camp were awake next morning before the yellow tints of sunrise had coloured the east. The messengers from Cinderford and Littledean had returned with promises of joyful and ready co-operation; those sent to Newnham would return in the train of Orcar.

About nine o'clock the besiegers formed up in the belt of trees in the same order as on the preceding day. By half-past nine the first flight of arrows came through the air with a hum and a whirr ! But no Saxon body presented itself for a target, and no missile discharge came in reply. The besiegers' screen of yesterday was now piled on the wall as a shelter for the besieged. Another volley was tried, and then another, but with like results ; walls and ramparts bristled with the feathery weapons and that was all.

Mortified and enraged the Welshmen came on with loud shouts. They reached the moat, and were throwing in their logs and branches as before, when suddenly a forest of heads rose above the ramparts, and a volley of arrows and spears, so well aimed and deadly, came therefrom, that the foremost line of besiegers retired hastily and in confusion. Another death-dealing shower followed them, and the ramparts were empty again.

Behind them, however, lurked every available man in the castle and every boy capable of drawing a bow or throwing a spear. The enemy retired a little farther, well out of bowshot, and de Tournay and the ap Morgans held a short council. The men, sullen and angry, and considerably thinned in numbers, stood around, watching their wounded companions writhing and stumbling at the edge of the moat. Some looked anxiously back towards the trees, hoping to see signs of the body dispatched against Cinderford an hour before sunrise.

However, they looked in vain, for the sturdy miners were also abroad betimes, and the mixed body of Welshmen and Normans had fallen carelessly into the midst of a watchful and eager foe, and were scattered abroad in small bodies and driven steadily riverwards.

The besiegers determined to advance again. The archers came forward to a good shooting distance and stood with bows half bent ready to cover the advance of the spearmen and men-at-arms. At the signal these dashed forward bearing the great heavy ladders, the pile of brushwood and pine-branches, some lighted torches, and a small raft it was intended to fix underneath the drawbridge as a hearthstone for their fire.

Again the Saxons rose above the walls and discharged their weapons. But this time the shower was less deadly and less sustained, for iron-headed messengers of death rattled around and upon them like hailstones, and many a man heard the dull thud of his comrade's body as it toppled from the wall dead or severely wounded.

The enemy were successful in their onslaught this time. Protected by the splendid shooting of their archers, they fixed their cumbrous ladders, they swarmed into the moat, and the thick smoke from their fire went curling upwards, blinding and suffocating the defenders above the gate.

Up the ladders they came, chiefs and men; they reached the top; the defenders hurled down the beams and stones upon those in the moat. With cut and thrust they drove the yelling and shrieking foe back. But they came on in increasing numbers, for the archers, finding they could no longer shoot without the risk of killing their own men, slung their bows and drew their swords and swarmed up to the desperate encounter. Men grappled with one another on the broad top of the wall, and Saxon and foeman fell with a resounding splash into the moat, locked in an embrace of death.

Side by side Gurth and Sir John fought with the energy of a desperate cause. Halford had singled out the Norman soldier Bertrand, and the two were fighting a death duel like gladiators. Halford's superior height and position told in the end, and the Norman went spinning from the battlements.

But underneath the drawbridge the fire crackled and roared; presently the ropes burnt through, and the structure fell with a crash across the moat. With shouts of victory the besiegers dashed along to the gate. The fiery raft was swept from underneath the bridge, and in a few moments another pile was blazing beneath the archway, and huge battering-rams were pounding away to aid the work of the fire.

Gurth sprang from the wall to meet this new danger. The assailants, cheered by success, fought with redoubled energy, and the Saxons struggled as men only struggle for hearth and home. It was an anxious moment, and Sir John glanced towards the trees in the hope of descrying help. None was yet discernible, and calling on Halford to join him he pressed along into the thickest of the conflict.

Before these two mighty arms the lighter-armed Welshmen gave way, and de Tournay himself dashed forward to stem any possible tide of retreat. But the Saxons battled on like lions, and, by a magnificent effort, cleared that part of the wall. But the smoke was coming in jets through the gate, and the rams thundered ceaselessly. It could not last much longer, and Gurth had massed a living wall of men to resist the inevitable rush of the enemy.

Just at this juncture a rousing cheer came from the walls, and an answering one, growing momentarily louder and louder, came from the Forest. The besiegers turned, and to their dismay saw two close bodies of fresh foes heading swiftly towards them.

Gurth sprang to the walls. Orcar saw him, and with a loud shout of "An Orcar!" "A Wulf!" came on with redoubled pace.

The young thane rushed to the gateway, the bolts

were withdrawn, the gate flew open, and the ready Saxons sprang across fire and bridge, brushed their enemies aside or drove them before them, and the fight was transferred to the open.

But the besiegers, though surprised, were not beaten. Shouting to the Welsh chieftains to array themselves against the newcomers, de Tournay rallied his Normans, who thus far had suffered but little loss, and faced round in readiness for the adversaries he most desired to meet. They, on their part, were not loth to grant him the encounter he awaited; with yell and shout they came on.

Gurth's intention was to engage de Tournay. So, finding Halford striding like his shadow beside him, he exclaimed, "Yon Norman is for me!"

"Ay," answered the giant laconically, "but I stand by!"

The young thane flushed; his follower's words seemed anticipatory of defeat. He set his teeth and determined this should not be. A dozen strides more, and the combatants met on all sides; the *mêlée* became general.

Gurth and the Norman knight fought their way towards each other and interchanged a few blows. Then the press separated them, but they soon came together again. Both were skilful swordsmen, and both were cool and determined. But, while the Norman fought to kill, the young Saxon fought to wound and disarm, for he was determined that de Tournay should hang like the cur he was; therefore he fought the more warily.

Gurth endeavoured to cut the Norman's sword from

his hand, but the blow fell short, and his adversary
lunging forward pierced his left shoulder to the bone.
The young thane staggered backwards, but, quickly
recovering himself, and smarting with pain, he leapt
with the agility of a veritable young wolf, full at his
foeman's throat. The point of his sword crashed
through the protecting rings of steel, and with a
choking cry the Norman fell. In a trice Halford was
astride the body, sweeping a clear ring round it
with his huge battle-axe. The Norman men-at-
arms hesitated for a moment, then broke and fled.
Mingling with their Welsh allies, they carried confusion and dismay with them, and the whole body of
the enemy, seized with panic, betook themselves to
headlong flight. The Welsh chieftains, endeavouring
to stem the frantic torrent, fell wounded into the
hands of the victorious Saxons.

Orcar and the men of Littledean and Newnham
pursued the broken array, killing some and taking
many prisoners, and of those who the previous day
had marched so jauntily to the attack, barely half
escaped into the sheltering depths of the Forest.

*　　*　　*　　*　　*

In spite of many missing voices and faces there was
high carousal in the halls of the Wulf that night.
And the gallant young chief of the house, his arm
swathed in bandages, sat a proud lord and victor at
the head of the table.

The great assemblage drank solemnly to the
memories of the dead, and spoke tenderly of them ;
they drank " wassail " to the wounded, and spoke words
of hope ; they drank " wassail " and " love " to their

young thane, and vowed that to die for him was a
pleasure and honour. And the Lady of the Dean
then and there laid down all authority at the feet of
her son, and every man uprose and swore a solemn
oath of homage to him.

Already men were whispering of Gurth's likeness to
his warlike father, and that the martial glories of the
Wulf were come again.

CHAPTER XII.

GILBERT DE TOURNAY did not die, for the good Lady of the Dean and Elgiva, forgetful of his past villainies, nursed him back to health. Neither was he hanged, a thing of scorn and reproach, from an oak in the forest. The two ladies having saved his life, claimed it, and Gurth could not refuse to acknowledge their claims. So the Norman, healed in more senses than one, set out one day in the sweet sunshine of April, his face set towards the gloomy and cheerless castle at Mitcheldean.

After he had been there for the space of a few days, he sent an escort to the Dean craving the presence of his two gentle nurses. He wished them to come unaccompanied by any friend or retainer. In spite of the remonstrances of Gurth and Sir John, who trusted the Norman as they would a scotched viper, they granted his request to the full, and set out with his men-at-arms for his ill-famed stronghold.

The knight received them with every courtesy, and with unfeigned pleasure and gentleness. He thanked them quietly and earnestly for the life they had doubly saved, and then gave Elgiva a packet, sealed and endorsed, instructing her to open it on

162

the morning when she became the bride of the thane
of Wulf. He then escorted them homewards until
the tower of Wulf Castle appeared amidst the trees.
Here he took an affectionate farewell of the two
women he had so persecuted, disappeared among the
trees, and his familiar form was seen in the Forest
no more.

The two wounded ap Morgans, with many of their
followers, were detained as prisoners of war ; but on
entering into a solemn undertaking to keep to their
own side of the Wye in future, their arms were
restored to them and they were permitted to depart
without further molestation. The young thane treated
his hereditary foes thus generously out of a desire to
put an end to these perpetual border wars ; he wished
his vassals to pursue their avocations of forestry,
herding, and mining in peace.

For nearly two years the Welshmen were true to
their compact, but eventually habit and instinct proved
stronger than oaths, and the foresters were once more
compelled to throw down mattock, axe, and spade,
and take to sword, and bow, and spear.

One glorious day in early May, amidst the singing
of the birds, the bursting of the buds, and the nodding
and curtseying of the woodland flowers, the whole
Forest took holiday. Horns rang merrily through
the glades, and youth and maid, and goodman and
wife, gammer and gaffer came forth to dance and sing
and make good cheer. For their beloved young thane·
was that day to marry the maiden of his heart and
theirs, and the sweet and gentle daughter of the
smith was, with great ceremony and rejoicing, to be

installed as mistress of the great and mighty house of the Wulf.

That night bonfires blazed on all the woodland heights, and men saw the reflections at Gloucester, where the worthy citizens gathered on the Cross and hurrahed for their illustrious fellow-townsman and his winsome daughter.

At the Dean all was happiness. And when at the wedding feast the bride opened the sealed packet of de Tournay, and it became known that he had made her a free gift of all his Forest domain, then men said that the sweet faces of their ladies were a power, even against the mightiest foes.

THE END.

Printed by Hazell, Watson, & Viney, Ld., London and Aylesbury.

www.ingramcontent.com/pod-product-compliance
Lightning Source LLC
Chambersburg PA
CBHW021113020726
47500CB00003B/734